Aspen's Defense

A Curvy Girl Hockey Romance

Nichole Rose

Nichole Rose

CONTENTS

About the Book

To win a shot with his curvy girl, this hockey hunk will become her best line of defense.

Aspen

Leaving home was the best decision I ever made.

Unfortunately, my older brother disagrees.

He thinks I still need someone to look after me.

I didn't expect him to send his former teammate to do his dirty work, though.

Noah Diamante, AHL superstar, won't leave me alone, and I like it a little too much.

Especially the part where he saves my life from a madman.

Now, he swears I'm never getting rid of him.

But does he mean it...or am I just a favor to him?

Noah

If anyone had told me that coffee would change my life, I would have laughed.

Right up until I set eyes on Aspen Whatley at the local coffee shop, anyway.

She's everything right in this world.

But she's a little spitfire, hellbent on taking on the world by herself.

Knowing her brother wants me to keep an eye on her doesn't earn me any points.

Until her life is on the line, and she has nowhere to turn.

Now, she's looking over her shoulder, and I'm pissed about it.

No one threatens what belongs to me.

But I've been playing defense my entire life.

I'll protect this goddess and make her mine.

You can bet on that.

Chapter One

Aspen

"A**spen!**"

I close my eyes with a groan as Jack Whitlock shouts my name, waving his arms over his head in a bid to get my attention. As if I didn't hear him yelling at me like the sky is falling. Everyone in The Golden Mug, the adorable little coffee shop where I work, heard him.

"Aspen!"

"Yes, Jack?"

"Why is there a delivery truck blocking half the parking lot?"

"Because you double-booked deliveries again." I contin-ue wiping down the counter as I speak. "Margot's Coffee is blocking the alley. Sean had nowhere else to park his truck."

Jack whips his dark head toward the back of the shop, his handsome face the picture of shock. "Shit. It's Tuesday?"

I pause mid-swipe, genuinely curious how the man functions when he doesn't even know what day it is half the time. Actually, I'm not sure he even knows what state he's in half the time. Jack Whitlock, like a large chunk of the population of Silver Spoon Falls, is a millionaire. Or a billionaire. Or whatever you call men with more zeroes in their bank accounts than they could ever hope to spend.

Unlike most, however, Jack does not always have his life together. It's a mystery to me how the man made millions—or billions—when he's a hot mess half the time. He has a brilliant mind, but he needs a keeper. He adamantly refuses to hire an assistant, however. He swears they just get in his way. How he made it to forty-one is a mystery.

"Don't answer that," he mutters, waving me off before I can ask how he lost track of the days this time. I'm not even sure I want to know what's got him distracted now. The list is long, my shift just started, and it's already been a day. "It's too early for you to give me shit."

"Who me?" I bat my lashes at him and stow my wash rag beneath the counter to pour him a cup of coffee. "Never have I ever given you crap that wasn't deserved."

"Right." He snorts, making me smile. The man may be a menace, but he's a great boss. He's also a friend. At least enough of one not to fire me when I inevitably upset a customer, which happens all too often around here.

I am not here to take abuse from the under-caffeinated and overly crabby. My mouth could never...and it often doesn't. But Jack shrugs off the complaints and tells whoever I've upset to be nicer to his staff or not to come back. Most come back. I make fantastic coffee and killer scones. Plus, this is the only coffee shop downtown. It works in our favor.

"I guess I'll go deal with inventory." Jack sighs dramatically.

"Don't you dare. The last time you tried to help with inventory, I couldn't find anything for days."

Jack lifts a brow, stripping off his biker jacket. "Don't you work for me?"

"Not for long," I remind him. I've finally saved enough to buy half of this place from him. Come this time next month, I'll be part owner of The Golden Mug, and Jack will have one less business to worry about. Eventually, I'll own the whole thing. Jack has already agreed to sell it to me when I'm ready. He actually offered to sell it to me on credit, but I refuse to take a handout from anyone. When the ink dries on the deal, I want to know it was because I earned it, not because it was given to me.

My brother, Nash, won't be thrilled when he finds out I plan to buy Jack out. I've been in Silver Spoon Falls for two years, and my brother still thinks I'm too young to be on my own. I know this because he tells me all the time. He's convinced I'm going to come running back home to Washington at any moment.

The world is too big for you, Aspen.

You belong at home where I can keep an eye on you, baby sis.

I'm moving you back home if you don't answer your phone, Aspen Marie.

I love my brother to death, don't get me wrong, but if I could legally beat him with a broom, some days, I think I would. He's always been my best friend. But he's also infuriatingly overprotective. I'm not the sad little girl who needs her big brother to protect her from bullies anymore, as much as he still likes to believe I am. And I'm not moving back in with him.

This is my home now. Texas is in my blood.

"Fine." Jack shakes his head, holding up his hands in surrender. "I'll just sit here and drink my coffee like a good boy and let you do all the work like usual." He swipes his cup off the counter and makes a show of taking a drink. "Why do I even bother coming here anymore?"

"Because there's a giant spider in the bathroom, and I am *not* dealing with it?"

"How big is giant?"

I hold my hands a foot apart to demonstrate. I may be exaggerating slightly, but not much. The thing is huge.

"Yeah, fuck that." Jack shudders. "I'm not dealing with it."

"Oh my god." I glare at him. "Why do you even bother coming here anymore?"

"Your guess is as good as mine." He smirks, swiping his cup from the counter to take a drink.

I take back everything I said. My boss sucks.

"**A**spen!"

"I swear to God, Jack," I growl, marching out of the stock room half an hour later. I drag the back of my hand across my forehead, pushing damp tendrils of hair out of my face. Why is it always so hot back there? "If you don't stop shouting my name like the freaking roof is on fire, I'm going to lose my ever-loving min..." I trail off, coming to a dead stop in the middle of the doorway as my gaze lands on Jack. Well, not on Jack but on the gorgeous man standing beside him.

Noah Diamante, AHL superstar. The man is drop-dead gorgeous. His olive skin and razor-sharp jawline are enough to make women do crazy things. And don't even get me started on his smoking hot body or those penetrating green eyes that make my stomach turn flips.

My brother has played hockey my entire life. None of his teammates ever gave me the butterflies until he played with Noah on the Yellowjackets a few years ago. Noah blew out his knee a few years into his NHL career and got sent down to their AHL team—the Yellowjackets—to recover. Unfortunately for me, Nash got called up to the Capitals, and we moved back to Washington before I ever got the chance to actually meet Noah, but I've been following his career ever since. I'd heard that he was making the move to Silver Spoon Falls to play for the Falcons. I might have even done a little happy dance.

But that was before Nash called to tell me he asked Noah to keep an eye on me. As if I haven't lived in this town on my own for the better part of two years. As if I want one of my brother's friends—even one who looks like Noah—meddling in my life. The absolute last thing I need is for Noah to report all my business to Nash.

He'll never leave me alone, then.

Dear Baby Jesus, is there a return policy on older brothers? Asking for a friend.

"There you are." Jack beams, oblivious to the fact that I've been rendered stupid at the sight of Noah in his tattered jeans and dark t-shirt. Seriously. Couldn't Nash have sent Quasimodo, at least? "Noah is here to see you."

Noah? *Noah*? Oh my God. How are they possibly on a first-name basis already? I wasn't in the stock room that long.

"Hey." Noah shoots me a grin. And hello, ovaries. Nice of you to join us. "You probably don't know who the fuck I am, but–"

"Noah Diamante, first-line left defenseman for the Falcons. You played hockey with my brother on the Yellowjackets during your first year on the team. You're consistently one of the top defensive players in the league, though you haven't managed to outscore Slaney yet." Why am I babbling? Mouth, please shut up.

"You know hockey," he says with an easy smile, clearly impressed. "Nice."

"It happens when your older brother plays," I mumble.

His smile grows. "I can see that. Nash said you knew your shit."

"What else did Nash say?" I'm not entirely sure I want to know. My brother knows all my dirty secrets...like the fact that I wanted to be a dragon when I was a kid, and about my humiliating Jane Austen era. I'm pretty sure I still have an entire diary full of thee's and thou's chronicling that period floating around somewhere. Don't even get me started on what Nash knows about my dating life. Considering that he's the reason I've never actually had one...well, let's just say he knows all the pitiful details.

"Not nearly enough," Noah mutters, his gaze flicking up and down my body.

I quickly cross my arms to hide my nipples, fairly certain he can see them through my uniform top since they're hard enough to cut glass at this point. His eyes heat and darken as he looks me over, turning my blood to liquid fire.

"He didn't tell me that you're fucking gorgeous. He also didn't tell me that hearing you talk hockey would get me all hot and bothered."

"Jesus Christ," Jack mumbles, scratching his face as if to hide a smile.

"You did not just say that." I gape at Noah, pretty sure he may have been dropped on his head as a baby.

"Uh, yeah. Not trying to be rude, but have you seen you?" He looks at me like I'm the one talking crazy here. "Nash didn't tell me that you look like a dirty little angel." He glances at Jack. "Shit. No offense or anything."

"None taken." Jack holds up his hands, smirking like the dang cat that ate the canary. I'm killing him. "Please, feel free to continue like I'm not even here."

"Oh my god," I whisper, glaring at my boss, who is practically choking on his tongue to keep from falling into a fit of laughter. This isn't the first time someone has hit on me at work. It happens more than I'd like. People seem to think that flirting with the barista is a sure way to get VIP treatment around here. They quickly learn that flattery will get them nowhere with me.

But Jack loves watching the show anyway. This is one show that needs to end soon, however. Noah may have starred in most of my fantasies for the last few years, but I'm not falling for his crap. No way. Not when I know he's reporting back to my brother.

"Where are we going to dinner tonight?"

"Excuse me?" I blink, caught off guard by the question.

"Dinner tonight," Noah repeats. "Where do you want to go after you show me around town?"

"Um, I am not showing you around town," I protest, gaping at him.

"You don't want to show me around?"

"Yes. No. I mean, I didn't agree to this." I huff out a breath, scraping my wild hair behind my ears as I try to regain my composure. Why did I even get out of bed this morning?

"Then we'll skip the tour and go straight to dinner. What time do you get off?"

I stare at Noah for a moment, trying to decide if I want to kill my brother now or make him suffer first. My crush is standing in front of me, talking about taking me to dinner...and we both know he's only doing it because Nash put him up to it.

"She gets off at five today."

"No, I don't." I cut my eyes at Jack. "Can you please go away? You aren't helping."

My boss backs away slowly, fighting laughter. The jerk.

"Look, I'm not sure why you owe my brother," I say to Noah once we're alone, "but you can just tell him that you're checking in and everything is great. No need to follow through. You two can call it even, and he'll never hear differently from me. But I do *not* need a babysitter, and we are not going to dinner."

Noah listens attentively to my little speech, nodding along. He gets it, thank God. I won't have to dodge him all over town just to keep him from reporting my every move to my crazy brother.

Note to self: murder Nash next time you see him. This is beyond too much.

"Do you feel better now that you've gotten that off your chest?"

"Surprisingly, yes."

Noah's deep chuckle does illegal things to forbidden places. "Good, because I'm not lying to your brother. I'm a man of my word, Dimples. Now, what time do you get off?"

"What time do I...what?" I splutter. He can't be serious!

His soft laughter rolls over me in a wave. "What time does your shift end, baby? I'll swing back by then to pick you up."

I gape at him, not sure if he's lost his mind or if I have. Did he not hear anything I said? "I'm not going anywhere with you," I growl. "I don't care what kind of favor you owe Nash. My life is my own."

"Good to know. I'll make sure to tell him that if he calls." Noah leans over the counter, his eyes locking on mine. "But I'll still be here when you get off."

Dear God, my brother sent a madman to babysit me.

CHAPTER TWO

Noah

Nash Whatley is an asshole beneath his nice guy exterior. He pretends he's a friend, but in actuality, he's a secret keeping, sister hiding bastard.

How did I not know his little sister was a goddess? Better yet, why didn't he warn me that I was about to walk right into my future?

Because he's an asshole, that's why.

As soon as I make it back to my truck, I send him a text telling him as much.

Me: You're an asshole.

I barely manage to start the truck before my phone rings.

"What did she do?" His growl echoes through the speakers.

"Hello to you, too." I smile, not surprised by his lack of greeting. Nash has no chill and no time to waste. He's been the same way for as long as I've known him. No one was surprised when he got called up to the NHL to take my place when their original replacement couldn't hack it. He's a beast with an iron will.

"What'd she do?" he repeats.

"It's what you did, fucker," I peer through the windshield at the coffee shop, hoping to catch a glimpse of her. She's fucking gorgeous. It's really no wonder he keeps her hidden when she looks like she does. Her auburn hair and green eyes are killer, especially paired with those dimples and her wicked curves. "You failed to tell me that she's pissed."

"I may have forgotten to mention that part," he mutters wearily. "I'm guessing she gave you nine kinds of hell?"

"Nothing I couldn't handle." I give up trying to see her through the tinted windows of the shop and put the truck in gear, pulling out onto the street. If I don't get my ass in gear, I'll be late to practice. "She seems to think you sent me to spy on her."

He doesn't say anything.

Well, shit.

"Fucking A, Nash," I groan. "Are you trying to piss her off and get me shivved?"

"She won't shiv you." He doesn't sound too certain about that.

"You asked me to look out for her, which I'm happy to do. But I draw the line at playing spy, man." There's no fucking way I'm reporting back to him. She's grown. If he wants to be in her business, that's his deal, not mine.

I need her to like me, not want to kill me on sight. Especially since she's going to have my babies and shit. We can't do that if she doesn't even like me, now can we? No, no, we can't.

Note to self: stop doing favors for people. It's how you wake up in Mexico with *Get Pucked* tattooed on your ass cheek.

That's exactly what happened last time I did our goalie, Atlas Jacks, a favor.

"I'm not asking you to spy on her," he finally says. "I just want to make sure she's all right." He blows out a breath. "She's up to something. She's been secretive as fuck lately."

"I've been in town five minutes." More like six weeks, but whatever. The point is, I haven't been here long enough to make enemies of the barista at the best coffee shop on the way to the arena. Especially the barista I'd like to fuck into next week. "Have you asked her what she's up to?"

"No. She won't tell me."

"How do you know if you haven't asked?"

"Do you have sisters?"

"Uh, fuck no." Thank God for small mercies. His sister is already giving me stress. I doubt sisters of my own would be any more cooperative.

"Trust me, she isn't telling me. She says I meddle too much. So she hides shit and doesn't tell me anything and tries to do everything on her own," he complains. "I need someone to tell me what the fuck she's doing."

"It ain't gonna be me."

"Why the fuck not?"

"Because your sister is gorgeous."

He growls a warning.

"She's also funny and feisty as hell," I continue, ignoring said warning. "I like her."

"Jesus fucking Christ."

"You're the one who asked me to keep an eye on her."

"I already regret it."

"No, you don't."

"Do so," he mutters like a two-year-old.

"You would have warned me to keep my goddamn hands to myself from the beginning if you wanted me to keep my goddamn hands to myself," I tell him. "You didn't warn me." Nash has this weird idea that he owes me because he took my spot on the Capitals. As if it's his fault I fucked up my knee, and they called him up to take my place. But the fact that he didn't warn me off his sister means he doesn't hate the idea of the two of us hitting it off. I know him well enough to know that much.

"I thought it went without saying," he growls. "She's my sister."

"Which is why I'm being honest with you now. I like her, and I'd like to get to know her. I can't do that if she thinks I'm spying for you."

"I could just tell her that you're spying for me," he points out. "Then she'll shiv you, and there won't be any getting to know anyone."

I scowl at the traffic light. Maybe I'll shiv him and save me and Aspen both a little trouble. "I begin to see why you get on her goddamn nerves."

He laughs quietly. "She loves me."

"You still annoy the hell out of her." I turn off Broadway, headed toward the arena.

"She calls it annoying. I call it worrying," he says. "I raised her. I figure I'm allowed."

I knew they were close, but I never realized he raised her. He's always been tight-lipped as fuck about her. All I knew was that he had a little sister, and he didn't bring her around the team. But I'm thirty-four, and Nash is only a few years younger than I am. Aspen may be young, but she isn't that much younger than us. "How old is she?"

"Twenty-two."

Shit. She's a helluva lot younger than I thought. Twelve years younger than I am.

He sighs. "She was eleven when our parents died. The wreck nearly took her too."

"Jesus." No wonder he's protective of her. He damn near lost everyone in one fell swoop. Which means I need to tread carefully. "Be straight with me, man. Is it going to be a problem with you if I get to know her?"

He hesitates for a long moment. "Is this you asking for permission to date my sister, Diamante?"

"This is me asking if you're going to have a problem with me dating your sister." I don't ask for permission. That's not his to give. It's her choice who she dates. But he's a friend. I owe him a heads-up, at the minimum. I don't want his approval to be one of the things standing between us when she's already suspicious of me. The last thing I need is one more obstacle standing in the way.

"Fucking hell," he growls. "I didn't ask you to watch her so you could get her into your bed."

"Give me a little credit here. You know me better than that." I don't fuck around. In fact, I've never fucked around. He's one of a handful of people who knows that. It's one of the reasons we bonded the few weeks we played together. He didn't party, and neither did I.

We were in the minority. Most of the guys on the team were more than happy to take a different bunny to bed every night. Nash and I were always the two who caught hell because we weren't fucking everything that moved. He had a sister to worry about, and I was busting ass trying to recover. Since then, I've been busting ass carving out a name for myself in the AHL. My NHL dreams may have gone up in smoke, but I'm still one of the highest-paid players in the AHL.

He laughs abruptly, a sound that makes me sweat a little. "Fine. You can try to get to know her if she'll let you," he says. "But good fucking luck with that."

"What does that mean?"

He laughs again instead of answering.

"What does that mean? Nash!"

The fucker hangs up on me.

"You're fucking Aspen?" Colter Bayliss, my best friend and teammate, gapes at me from the bench, a skate blade dangling from his hands. "Since fucking when?"

"That isn't remotely close to what I said," I mutter, shaking my head.

"He said she's the barista he wants to fuck."

I shoot a dirty scowl at Atlas, our goalie, who just smirks at me and continues strapping on his pads. Reid Lawless snickers, so I turn a scowl on him, too. I swear to God, whoever put together this roster stacked it with idiots.

"I didn't say that either," I growl. "I asked what you guys know about her."

"And the only reason you're asking is because you're interested." Miles Tempest doesn't even look up from his phone. "You want to sleep with her."

Well...obviously. But I'm not telling any of these morons that. They're less than helpful already. The last thing I need is for them to show up at the coffee shop every day to bug the shit out of her. She'll never give me the time of day then. Considering Nash's ominous warning and her less-than-enthusiastic response to spending time with me, I'm guessing bombarding her with these idiots will not help my case any.

"She's a badass."

I glance up at Jenson Sparks. Finally, someone helpful. "You know her?"

"Not much, but I've spent some time at the shop," he says, spearing me with an amused look. "You sure you want to pursue her?"

"Why do you ask?" I growl, feeling defensive.

"Because she does not take shit from anyone." He flicks his gaze up and down me, his smile growing. "Especially guys like you."

"What the fuck does that mean?" I demand, narrowing my eyes on him.

"He means pretty boys," Reid says through laughter.

I flip them both off. They've been calling me that shit for the last six weeks, thanks to some elderly lady in town who took one look at me and cooed, "Oh, he's a pretty one. I might just have to start watching this hockey business if they make them like him.".

The biker with her just shook his head and looked at me as if to say he wasn't responsible for the shit that comes out of her mouth.

"I mean charming motherfuckers," Jenson says. "Every once in a while, some suave motherfucker will try to flirt with her at the counter, but she shuts it down quickly and mercilessly. They end up with hurt feelings, even though everyone should know by now not to even try it." He gives me a pointed look.

"I haven't tried anything."

He snorts his disbelief.

"Nash asked me to look after her."

"My sister read that book before," Devlin Ramsey says from the far end of the bench. "It ends with fucking and the brother pissed."

"For fuck's sake," I growl, throwing up my hands. "I'm never asking you guys anything ever again. You're useless."

"I'm not useless," Reid protests. "I know Aspen."

I narrow my gaze on him, not sure if he's bullshitting me or not.

"I'm serious. She and my wife are friends."

"What do you know about her?" Jenson asks.

Reid flicks his gray eyes in my direction before smirking at Jenson. "I know this motherfucker doesn't stand a chance. She's going to eat him alive."

The rest of my teammates crack up laughing.

I shoot him a disgusted look and flip them off. They may be betting against me, but I'm not. If I have to fight fire with fire to claim her, so be it. But one way or another, Aspen will be mine. I won't give up until she surrenders every little piece of herself to me. Starting with her secrets.

Because Nash was right about one thing. She is up to something. It's the only reason I can figure that she's so adamant about not wanting me around. I just need to convince her that she can trust me not to go running to Nash. That should be easy enough...right?

"You're kidding me," Aspen growls ten minutes before the shop closes, her hands propped on her luscious hips as she spears me with a dark look. "I thought we agreed you weren't coming back today."

"Did we? Huh. I must have forgotten," I lie cheerfully, sliding onto a stool in front of her. "But since I'm here now..." I place the to-go bag on the counter in front of me. "We might as well have dinner together."

She flicks her gaze to the bag and then back to me, spluttering.

Fuck, she's cute when she's pissed. Her eyes practically shoot fire at me, and her cheeks flush a deep pink. Why anyone is intimidated by her, I don't know. She may have claws, but she's a harmless little kitten.

"You didn't forget at all, did you?" she accuses, her hands still planted on her wide hips.

"Nope. Told you I'd be here when you got off."

She hits me with a withering glare that makes my dick hard. "You're taking this entirely too far, Noah. I don't need a babysitter!"

"I'm not here to babysit you, Dimples. I'm here to have dinner with you." I tap the to-go bag for emphasis. "I wasn't sure what you liked so I called Nash. He suggested Broadway Steakhouse."

"You called Nash?" She gapes at me like I've grown a third head.

"Twice, actually." I slide the bag across the counter toward her, holding her gaze. "The first time, I let him know that I would not be spying for him."

"You...what?"

"He was cranky about it, but he wasn't entirely surprised." I slip plastic utensils out of my pocket and place them on top of the bag. "He wasn't even surprised when I told him that I think you're gorgeous."

For the first time since I met her, she actually cracks a smile. "You told him that?"

"Mmhmm."

"And he isn't flying here right now?"

"Might be." I shrug. "I didn't ask."

She stares at me for a long, silent moment, then shakes her head, her tense stance easing. "You're a crazy person, Noah Diamante; I hope you know that."

"Does that mean you're having dinner with me?"

"Yes."

I grin.

"But only because I'm hungry," she quickly adds.

CHAPTER THREE

Aspen

"H oly shit." Noah's gaze flies to mine, his eyes wide.

"I told you," I say through laughter. "They're amazing."

He chews the blueberry scone before swallowing. "Fuck me. You make these?"

"Every morning."

"No wonder this place is always packed when I drive by," he says, staring at the crumbs on the plate I just set in front of him. "That's fucking amazing."

"It was my mom's recipe."

"Yeah?"

I nod, not sure why I'm telling him this. Maybe because talking is less awkward than him staring at me. He did that the first ten minutes of dinner. I think he would have kept doing it had I not started chattering. He's...intense. Or maybe it's simply that I'm intensely attracted to him. Either way, my panties are soaked, and it's his fault.

I'm determined to keep my distance since he's here as a favor to Nash, but he's so outrageous, it's endearing. Most guys get mad when you tell them no. They get offended that you dared to reject them. I can't count how many times I've been called a bitch for declining an offer I didn't ask for in the first place. Or how many times I've been told I'm not actually their type and they were just being nice. As if the fact that I'm plus size means I'm somehow unworthy. Miss me with that mess. I may be a big girl, but I learned a long time ago that fat doesn't mean ugly, and thin doesn't mean beautiful.

I was bullied a lot when I was younger. When you're chubby, and you're named after a tree, kids get inventive with the name-calling. I was Fat Forest for a while, or Bigger Than an Aspen. The ones doing the name-calling were usually thin. I'm not sure why they made me their target—maybe because I was the girl with no parents. But it taught me that people say a lot of mean crap when they're jealous. Hurt people hurt people, and insecure people love to lash out.

Rejected men are the worst. They do an about-face fast enough to cause whiplash. One minute, you're a goddess.

The next, they were just doing you a favor because no one would ever possibly date someone your size. Ugh.

Noah is a refreshing change from the norm. Despite my rejecting him, he hasn't gotten nasty or passive-aggressive. He hasn't been rude. No matter what I say, he just comes back for more. Every word he says is more outrageous than the last. I've met charming men before. They're everywhere around here. But I'm in serious danger of softening toward this one.

I'll worry about that later.

"She taught you how to cook?"

"No," I murmur sadly, a lump forming in my throat. "She died before she got the chance, but I have all of her recipes. One day, this place will be half bakery, half coffee shop, using her recipes." I bite my lip as soon as I say the words. Crap. I shouldn't have told him that. If he's lying about telling Nash that he isn't going to spy for him, then my brother is going to know that I'm up to something. He'll be on my doorstep, demanding I move back home and driving me crazy.

"She ran a bakery?"

"Her and my dad ran two of them."

"I'm sorry you lost them so young," he says quietly, his voice sincere. "I'm damn glad the accident didn't take you too."

I look at him in genuine surprise. "Nash told you?"

He nods. "Always knew he had a sister, but I didn't realize he raised you."

"Yeah. He took custody of me after the accident so I didn't end up in foster care." He was barely out of college and was expected to go straight to the NHL. He ended up skipping the draft that year. Everything was so fresh and raw. I don't think he had the energy to expend in caring for me and tackling a professional career simultaneously.

I was in the hospital for a while. I broke my leg in three places, broke my arm, three ribs, and my collarbone. Nash was by my side through all of it, sacrificing everything to be there for me. By the time I healed enough for him to refocus on hockey, he couldn't find a team willing to sign him. It took him another two years before he finally went into the AHL on a two-way contract, with no guarantee that he'd ever see ice time in the NHL. I felt so guilty that he gave up his one shot, but he never complained.

When he was called up to the Capitals not long after joining the Yellowjackets, I felt better because he was meant to play hockey professionally. I guess it's part of the reason I'm so adamant about living on my own. He's sacrificed enough for me already. It's beyond time for him to have a life of his own.

"He's a good man."

"He is," I agree without hesitation. Nash may drive me insane, but he's the best brother. I know he's only over-protective because he worries. He almost lost me once. He never wants to go through that again, so he does everything he can to ensure it never happens. I just wish he'd worry a little less about me and more about himself. I love it right here in Silver Spoon Falls in my tiny little house. It's time for Nash to worry about Nash.

"You going to let me watch you make these if I come by in the morning?" Noah asks, changing subjects. He holds up a scone to illustrate what he means.

"You want to watch me bake?" I eye him critically.

"Why the fuck not?"

"Because I start at four in the morning?"

He blinks. "You're shitting me."

"Nope."

"How the fuck do you even function at four in the morning?"

I purse my lips and widen my eyes, looking around the shop.

"Point taken, smartass," he chuckles. "I'll be here." His gaze runs down my body. "Especially if I get to see you in a sexy little apron."

I try to ignore the heated look and his teasing comment. *Calm down, ovaries. He probably flirts with everyone like this.*

If I keep telling myself the same thing, maybe it'll sink in, and my heart won't turn flips every time he says something flirty to me. He looks like a Greek God, for crying out loud. I highly doubt the thought of me in an apron excites him.

I don't lack confidence, but I'm not delusional, either. Men who look like him date supermodels, not plus-size baristas with zero dating history and overprotective older brothers. That's simply the way the world works.

"What kind of favor do you owe my brother?" I ask after he demolishes the last two scones on the plate. He eats like my brother...which is to say like a bottomless pit. It happens when you spend half of every day working out or skating.

"Who says I owe your brother a favor?" He pops his thumb into his mouth, licking off icing.

My stomach clenches. I want to be that thumb right now...

"You're here doing his dirty work, aren't you?" I gather up our containers, trying not to think about his thumb or his mouth or the way my clit throbs faintly. Sweet baby Jesus, have mercy. I may kill my brother for this alone.

"There's nothing dirty about it." He smirks, watching as I shove the containers into the takeout bag on the table where he moved us to eat. "Not yet anyway, but we can certainly arrange that if dirty is what you want."

"My point is," I say loudly, ignoring his offer. "You're willingly offering to get up at four in the morning to watch me bake in the tiniest kitchen known to mankind. Seems to me if you don't owe Nash, you're insane."

"I'm always up early."

I make a sound in the back of my throat. He may be up early, but I doubt he's making a habit of watching women bake at four in the morning. He gets up early because his job demands it.

"Maybe I have a thing for his sister," he says.

"And maybe it's time for you to go home."

He reaches out, snagging my wrist as soon as I stand up. Before I can pull away, he's reeling me toward him around the side of the small table. I end up pressed up against his thigh, staring into his eyes. My heart pounds against my ribcage. I feel it in my throat, pulsing wildly.

His eyes are so damn green, and he is so damn handsome. Good grief. Standing next to him really is like standing next to a god. Only he's far too corporeal and *real* to be some ethereal entity. His body feels like a furnace against mine. He smells like pine soap and the sweet treat he just ate.

He tips my head down with a finger beneath my chin, forcing me to meet his gaze. I fight like hell not to get lost in his eyes. Fight like hell to remember that Nash sent him here. Except I don't want to remember it in this moment. I want to throw caution to the wind and kiss this man.

"Why is it so hard for you to believe I have a thing for you?" he asks, searching my face.

Because I've been dreaming about you for years.

Because you may be the only person on the planet capable of crushing my heart.

Because I'm not nearly as brave as I look.

All three are equally true, but I don't voice any of those truths. I give voice only to the fourth, equally valid reason he makes me nervous as hell.

"Because I know my brother," I mutter. "Nash never gives up when he wants something. And I know how much he wants me back home." He's only been trying since the moment I moved to Silver Spoon Falls.

"Maybe he's changed his mind."

"If you believe that, then you don't know my brother very well."

"People change."

"Nash isn't people. He's Nash. He wants you to help convince me to go home."

Noah doesn't deny it. I think we both know he can't.

I duck under his arm, putting space between us. "Like I told you this morning, you can save yourself the trouble and just tell him that you're checking in. I won't tell him any different. But I'm not going home, and I don't need you in my space, trying to sway me to the Darkside."

"If you think you're getting rid of me that easily, think again," he calls softly. "I'm not going anywhere until I convince you that I'm right where I want to be."

"You're definitely going somewhere, Noah," I say, grabbing my bag from behind the counter. "*Home.*"

I need a long soak and a glass of wine.

I spin around with my bag, only to bump into Noah. He grabs my shoulders to keep me from tumbling over backward.

"Sorry. I thought you heard me following you."

"No." I scowl up at him. "You move like a freaking ninja."

His smile makes my stomach turn flips again. "My bad." He watches me for a moment, his hands still clamped lightly on my shoulders, and then he shakes his head. "Fucking gorgeous," he growls, leaning down. His lips brush mine in a featherlight kiss that sends shockwaves all the way into my soul.

I think he feels them, too. He groans softly, and then slowly pulls back.

"You kissed me," I blurt, staring at him.

"Mmhmm." He tucks a strand of hair behind my ear, grins, and strolls toward the door. "See you in the morning, Dimples."

I gape after him, my fingers pressed to my lips and my mind wheeling. I think I'm going to need more than a glass of wine tonight.

CHAPTER FOUR

Noah

Sleeping is virtually impossible when an auburn goddess decides to take up residence in your brain. I toss and turn all fucking night, trying to get comfortable with a raging hard-on that refuses to abate. Every damn time he starts to go down, something about her pops into my head, and I'm rock-hard all over again.

I refuse to take care of the situation, though. I'm not getting off again until I'm getting her off. I'm a glutton for punishment, what can I say? Around two-thirty, I hit the gym and try to run off a little sexual frustration before I spend the morning at the shop with her. I'd rather her not shiv me when I toss her sexy ass up on the counter and try to eat her.

Call me crazy, but I don't think we're quite there yet. She may have opened up a little last night, but she still doesn't trust me or my motives. I could cheerfully thrash her brother right now. She's so damn stressed about him trying to meddle that she's not willing to entertain the possibility that I'm not on his side here. I get it. Really, I do. As far as she knows, my loyalty is to him, not her. But I have every intention of changing her mind on that front.

I'm not sure why he wants her back home so badly. Actually, that's not true. He misses the fuck out of her. She's his little sister, and half the United States stretches between them. I'd worry if I were in his shoes. But this is Silver Spoon Falls, home to the richest of the rich in Texas. It's not exactly a crime-riddled city or a den of inequity. She's safer here than she is in Seattle.

At a few minutes after three, I shoot Aspen a text.

Me: Good morning, Dimples.

I don't have to wait long to find out if she's been tossing and turning all night too. Within seconds, three little dots appear, letting me know she's already up.

Dimples: How'd you get my number??

Me: I would tell you but...

Dimples: Nash.

Me: Maybe. Maybe not.

Dimples: I should just start giving his number to random puck bunnies.

I chuckle, dragging a shirt on over my head.

Me: So I'm on the same level as a random puck bunny, huh? Ouch.

Dimples: Oops?

I laugh quietly, shaking my head. Fuck. I love that she doesn't give an inch without being a mean girl about it. She's cheeky and sassy without crossing the line.

Me: I have so many inappropriate comments now...

Dimples: Of course you do. I bet they all involve big sticks too, don't they?

Me: Maybe I'll tell you when I get there. Are we still on for this morning?

Dimples: I guess so.

Me: Wow. Even through text, I hear the reluctance.

Dimples: I guess so! Is that better?

Me: See you soon, baby.

I'm grinning from ear to ear as I slip my phone into my pocket and sit on the edge of the bed to pull on a pair of shoes. I've never been this fucking thrilled to be up at three in the morning in my life.

By three-thirty, I'm in the truck, headed toward downtown. I'm the only car on the road. Despite the late hour, it's still humid out. October in Texas is not like October in the Pacific Northwest. The heat just pools in the atmosphere here. Last month, it felt as if we were drinking it. It's cooling off now that fall is beginning to take hold, but it's still hot.

My phone rings halfway to the coffee shop. My smile grows when I see Aspen's number light up on my navigation screen.

"You miss talking to me already, Dimples?"

Her panicked breathing is the only response.

A jolt goes through me. The smile slides from my face. "Aspen? What's wrong?"

"There's someone in the coffee shop," she whimpers. "They broke in through the back."

My heart fucking stops. For a protracted moment, it simply ceases to beat. I stop breathing. Everything inside of me shrivels as pure terror for her takes over. Someone is in the shop, and she's there alone.

Fuck.

I hit the gas. The engine revs, the tachometer and the speedometer shooting upward.

"I'm on my way," I promise. "I'll be there in three minutes, tops. Can you stay hidden and hang on until then?"

"I don't know," she whispers, her voice barely audible. "S-should I try to scare them off?"

"No. Fuck no," I growl. "Don't let them know you're there if you can help it." I may not know much about crime and criminals, but I know enough to know revealing that she's in the shop right now is the absolute wrong thing to do. Maybe it'll scare them off. Or maybe they'll decide to hurt her. That's not a gamble I'm willing to take.

Fuck my life. Not even an hour ago, I was convincing myself that she's safer here than in Seattle. If this is the universe's way of telling me to get with the program and do what Nash wants...it's a mighty powerful goddamn lesson.

"But..."

"I will spank your gorgeous ass if you put yourself in harm's way, Aspen." My hands tighten around the steering wheel. I push the truck harder, flying through a red light at ninety miles an hour. If anyone from the Sheriff's Office is out running radar, they're just going to have to chase me to the coffee shop to write me a ticket because I hear the fear bleeding out of her tone as indignation and anger move in.

Her first instinct was to flee. Her second is to fight. She's offended that they're stealing what doesn't belong to them. And she's pissed that she feels helpless. I haven't known her long, but I know her well enough to know one thing she doesn't do is helpless. Aspen is a fighter, the kind of woman who takes charge of her own destiny, and gets shit done.

She's going to grow more and more indignant the longer she thinks about the fact that she's hiding while someone ransacks the shop she loves. I need to get there before she has time to dwell on it for too much longer. Otherwise, God only knows what she's going to do.

"I didn't say I was going to do that," she huffs at me. "But should I try to get a look at...?" A loud clatter sounds down the line, far too fucking close for comfort. She knocked something over. There's no way whoever is in there didn't hear it. I still hear whatever it is rattling across the goddamn floor.

A male's voice sounds in the background, faint and far away, as if he's in another part of the shop, but still loud enough to set my teeth on edge. He definitely heard whatever she knocked over.

"Run," I growl at Aspen. "Now. Get outside as fast as you can."

Her acknowledgment is a soft sob.

I fly around the corner onto Broadway, my tires screeching. The shop is six blocks away. Six blocks. It feels like ten miles.

"Hey!"

My blood runs cold as the same voice from earlier shouts. Aspen sobs, a devastatingly frightened sound that'll haunt my nightmares. So will the sound that follows. A loud explosion blasts down the line.

Aspen screams as glass erupts into the roadway down the street.

Jesus Christ. He has a gun.

"Aspen!" I shout, panic clawing at me.

She doesn't say anything. For what feels like an eternity, all I hear is chaos coming down the line, none of the sounds truly discernible. They're just a mishmash of distorted shuffles and muffled thumps and shattering items. I don't hear Aspen at all. I don't hear the motherfucker with the gun, either.

And then, Aspen stumbles through the front door of the shop and immediately begins running down the sidewalk. I don't know if she sees my truck or if it's instinct, but she races toward me, waving her hands over her head as if to get my attention.

I suck in a breath, relief coursing through me in a powerful wave. My gaze shifts past her to the shop, checking to see if the bastard inside follows her. But if he's still in there, he doesn't come running out after her. I slam on the brakes beside her and pop the locks.

She immediately races toward the passenger side and clambers in. She's pale and trembling. Tears streak down her face. I want to drag her into my arms, but I need to get her to safety first. Right now, that's what matters most.

"Hold on," I mutter, throwing the truck in reverse.

I hit the gas and reverse to the next street before straightening out. I head straight for the Sheriff's Office. Aspen sits beside me, breathing hard and shaking.

"Talk to me, baby. Are you hurt?"

"N-no," she whispers, her voice shaking. "He s-shot at me, but he m-missed."

I clench my jaw so hard it pulses. Everything in me demands I get her to safety, go back, and kill the son of a bitch. He tried to fucking shoot her. Jesus Christ. He deserves a slow, painful death for that. But even if I go back, chances are he's long gone by now. I'm guessing he ran as soon as she made it out of the shop.

It takes less than three minutes to make it to the Sheriff's Office. I pull right up to the doors before slamming the truck into park. Aspen's still pale and trembling, tears slipping down her cheeks. I hop out and circle around the truck to her.

"Come on, Dimples," I murmur, gently sliding her out of the truck. She's ice-cold and moving too slow. Is she going into shock? Fuck.

I tip her head back, catching a glimpse of the tears shimmering in her lashes. Even scared out of her mind, she's the prettiest little thing I've ever seen. And I could have lost her before I ever even had her.

"Don't slap me." I lay claim to her mouth in a searing kiss, trying to shock her back into reality. Maybe it's a dick move. I don't know. All I know is that she's too cold, and kissing her last night seemed to illicit a response from her. I figure it's the fastest way to do the same thing now.

I'd be lying if I said I didn't want to kiss her for me, too. Just because she's here and she's safe, and this has been the longest goddamn morning of my life. From the moment the phone rang until right this second feels like an eternity. Fear isn't something I'm used to feeling. It's not something I come up against often. But I felt it for her. More strongly than I've ever felt it before.

Especially when I heard that gunshot.

She gasps against my lips, her entire body jolting. And then her arms slide up around my neck. Thank God. I hold the kiss for a moment longer before breaking it. I could kiss her forever but now isn't really the time. And this wasn't really about that.

"T-thank you," she whispers after a moment.

"Did you just thank me for kissing you?"

She's definitely not at risk of going into shock now. She rolls her eyes at me. "Ugh, no."

I choke on a laugh, reaching into the back to grab one of my jerseys.

"What are you doing?" She swats at my hands when I try to pull it on over her head.

"You're ice cold, Aspen. We need to warm you up to make sure you don't go into shock."

"Oh." A pretty blush creeps across her cheeks as she takes the jersey, pulling it on over her head.

I watch her intently, trying to gauge how she's feeling. She's still pale and trembling, but she isn't crying now. The tears are already drying on her cheeks. Nash may worry about her, but she's strong as hell.

Fuck my life. Nash. He's going to lose his damn mind when he finds out about this. And it's not like I can't tell him. His sister was nearly shot. That's not something I can keep to myself. It's not something I *should* keep to myself.

But that's a problem for another day.

"Come on." I place my hand on the small of her back, leading her toward the doors of the Sheriff's Office. "Let's go rally the troops."

Aspen

Sheriff Dillon Armstrong isn't a morning person. Or maybe he isn't an armed robbery person. I'm not sure, but he's cranky. I'm feeling a little stabby myself, truth be told. I barely slept all night, thanks to a certain hockey player invading my dreams.

In them, dinner didn't end with him giving me a chaste kiss and me kicking him out of the shop. Oh no, it didn't. Things got downright pornographic. There was icing involved and everything. I finally gave up trying to sleep and took a lukewarm shower at 2:30.

Everything since has been what I think people call a shit show.

"Run through it again," Dillon says, scrubbing his hands through his messy hair. "What time did you get here?"

"Seriously?" Noah glares at him. "She's already been through it twice."

"And I need her to go through it again. It's not even five in the morning. I'm half awake."

Noah mutters a curse under his breath.

"Don't make me make you wait outside, Diamante," Dillon barks at him. "I'm not in the mood for this shit."

"I'm not waiting outside," Noah growls.

"It's fine." I place a hand on his arm, trying to keep the peace. Dillon is just trying to do his job, and Noah's just trying to look out for me. Neither of them is wrong here, and we're all on the same side. "I don't mind going through it again."

"This is the last time," Dillon says, glancing between me and Noah. "I just need to ensure I have all the facts straight."

"I got to the shop at 3:30," I start, leaving out the part about getting there early in the hopes that I'd finish early and have to spend less time in the kitchen with Noah. Either the universe hates me, or it's sending flaming arrows my way, trying to point me toward the gorgeous hockey player because my brilliant plan worked a little too well. We haven't spent a single second in the kitchen...but he's glued to my side anyway. "I barely made it around the counter when I heard someone rummaging around in Jack's office. I thought it was him."

"Wasn't me," Jack mutters.

"Really? You mean you aren't the one who tried to shoot me?"

He narrows his eyes at me and then cracks a smile. "Smartass."

"Why'd you think it was Jack?" Dillion asks.

"Because they were in his office?"

"Were there lights on?"

"No. That's why I didn't yell to ask why he was here so early."

Dillon nods, jotting something in his little notebook. Or maybe he's doodling, I don't know. What do cops write in those things anyway? "And then what happened?"

"The two men in the office started talking."

"What were they saying?"

"Look in there," I repeat. "You know this rich mothertrucker probably leaves money in the desk drawers."

"He called me a mothertrucker?" Amusement carves little lines around Jack's eyes. Even though the situation is serious, he can't help but tease me. I think he's trying to make me feel better. I know he feels terrible, though. He rushed here as soon as Dillon called him.

"No, he called you the expletive version," I mutter. "I edited to spare your one feeling."

"That's more like it," Jack mutters.

Even Noah relaxes a little bit, some of the tension flowing from him.

"What happened from there, Aspen?" Dillon asks, trying to get us back on track.

"I hid and called Noah." His number was the first one that came up on my phone. At least, that's what I'm telling myself. I don't have the mental energy to expend having a crisis over why I chose to call him out of everyone in my contacts. "Somehow, I knocked a coffee canister off the counter when I was trying to shift positions so I could try to at least get a look at whoever was in the shop if they came close to me."

Noah grunts beside me. He's made the same exact sound every single time we've gone over this. He's really not happy that I tried to see the guys in the office. I thought it was the smart thing to do, though.

Spoiler alert: It was a stupid thing to do!

As soon as the coffee canister hit the floor, my life flashed before my eyes. It flashed again when the two men burst out of the office, and I saw the gun. And again when the shot exploded the window beside my head.

Everything after that is a little bit of a blur. I remember feeling immensely relieved when I saw Noah. And I remember the feel of his lips on mine, searing me to my soul. But the rest of it? It's a little jumbled up and chaotic, as if the world fell out of focus for a while there and is only now beginning to right itself.

"Do you remember anything about what they look like?" Dillon asks.

I glance up at him. "I remember what they look like." That part isn't jumbled or chaotic. Their faces are seared into my brain. "The one with the gun was a few inches taller than me. He had red hair. I couldn't tell his eye color, but I'm pretty sure he had freckles. He seemed young, mid-twenties, maybe. I didn't see the other one very well, but he was about your height and lean, with short, dark-colored hair."

Dillon jots the entire time I talk and then looks at me. "Did you recognize either of them?"

"Possibly?" I shrug, uncertain. "The tall one seemed familiar, but I see a lot of people through here every day. It's possible he's been in here before, but not often enough for me to immediately recognize him in the dark. It was more just that he seemed familiar. Does that make sense?"

Dillon nods and then glances at Jack. "Do either of them sound familiar to you?"

"Possibly," he says, a troubled look on his face. "Before Aspen started, I had an employee here for a brief time, Glenda Brennan. Her son, Silar, has red hair and freckles. He was the reason I ended up having to let her go. He caused some trouble around here and she kept letting him come back."

"Shit," Dillon growls.

"You're familiar with him," Noah says. It's not a question.

Dillon nods reluctantly. "His name just crossed my desk last month on a list of new parolees from TDJC."

"He was in prison?" Noah growls.

"For a home invasion."

"Jesus fucking Christ."

"Would you recognize him if you saw him again?" Dillon asks me, his tone grim. His expression matches. I think his bad mood is getting worse.

"Yes."

"I'll scrounge up a photo and run it by for you to take a look at. If he's our guy, we'll start rattling cages until we shake him loose. I doubt he's gone far."

"She'll be staying with me," Noah says.

"Uh, no, she won't," I say.

"Yeah, you will. You aren't staying alone after what just happened. If they saw you, they may very well try to finish the job," Noah says, his expression implacable. "So you're either staying at my place, or I'm staying at yours. Either way, you aren't staying alone."

I glance to Jack for help.

"Don't look at me," my traitor of a boss says. "Your brother will have a shit fit if I let you stay with me, and that's drama I don't need right now."

Crap. Nash. He's going to lose his mind when he finds out about this, and there's no way he isn't going to find out. Even if I manage to convince Noah not to tell him, it'll get back to him eventually. I don't know how, but he always seems to know when something bad happens. It's like his freaking superpower or something.

"I'll stay with you on one condition," I tell Noah, hoping to forestall the inevitable for as long as humanly possible.

Noah's expression is rife with suspicion as he eyes me. "What's your condition, Dimples?"

"You can't tell my brother about what happened until after the sheriff finds and arrests his suspects." It won't keep Nash from finding out for long, but hopefully, long enough for the dust to settle. By the time I have to tell him the truth, the worst will be over, and there will be no reason for him to come swooping in to try to convince me to move back to Seattle.

I'll be able to buy half of the coffee shop, and then deal with him.

"You want me to lie to your brother," Noah says, searching my expression.

"I don't want you to lie," I say carefully. "I just want you to not mention it yet. That's all."

Dillon snorts softly. I shoot him a death glare. Sheriff or not, I still make his coffee and the scones he takes to Jules when he has to work late. He can be Team Aspen this once.

"Fine," Noah agrees. "I won't tell him. Yet."

"I'd like the record to reflect that I had nothing to do with this," Jack says.

"Uh, yeah, you do. Because you aren't telling him either." I cut my eyes at Jack. "Otherwise, I'm taking the day off while you deal with replacing the window and all the cranky customers."

Jack's eyes widen. "You wouldn't."

I eye him levelly.

"Well, now you're just being mean," he mutters.

I end up taking the day off anyway. Noah and Jack don't really give me much choice. They gang up on me and basically demand that I take the day off while the cleaning crew handles putting the shop back in order. Half an hour after the police clear out, I'm back in my car, headed home with Noah following behind me.

Brick meets us at the front door, meowing.

"Jesus Christ," Noah mutters. "That's the biggest cat I've ever seen."

I smile despite myself. Brick is massive. He appeared in my kitchen not long after I moved in. I have no idea where he came from, but no one ever does with the Cat Delivery System. It's just how the system works. He decided my house was his house and never left.

"You have to watch out for him," I warn Noah. "He's kind of shady."

"Aren't all cats?" Noah kneels down, extending a hand toward Brick.

Brick eyes him sideways for a minute, sniffs him, and then decides he's okay. He rubs against his hand, purring. Noah grins and scratches his ears.

"He has food issues," I murmur. "It doesn't matter where I hide the bag, he finds it. He's gotten into the pantry, my closet, the bathroom, the fridge..." I tick off the list on my fingers. "He's Houdini."

"He likes to eat."

"Until he can't hold anymore." He's so chonky, his belly practically drags the ground. "He's been on a diet for the last year, but he's very dramatic about it. I think maybe he broke into my house because he was starving."

Noah glances up at me, startled. "He broke into your house?"

"Yep. I came home from work, and he was hanging out in my kitchen."

"You're shitting me."

"I'm not." I laugh quietly at the shocked look on his face. "You haven't spent a lot of time around cats, have you?"

"Not criminal cats, no."

"I told you he was shady." I drop my keys in the bowl beside the door and head toward the back of the house. "I'm going to pack a bag, I guess."

"Where's Brick's stuff?"

I pause, turning to Noah in surprise. "You want to take Brick?"

"He can't stay here alone."

"It's only for the night..."

Noah's shaking his head before I even finish the sentence. "We don't know how long it'll take the sheriff to find these fuckers. It could be a while. You may need to stay with me for a while."

"I can't just move in with you, Noah." I gape at him. "I have things."

"I see that," he murmurs, scanning my living room. "Your shit will be fine, baby."

"Stuff."

A smile dances across his face. "Your stuff will be fine, baby."

"Stop calling me that."

"Whatever you say, baby."

"Oh my God," I groan, throwing my hands up. Next time I see Nash, I'm going to run him over with a Zamboni for sending this man to babysit me. He's impossible. And the more time I spend with him, the more I think *impossible* may be exactly what I like best. He's so freaking unflappable about it. It doesn't matter if I'm rejecting him or telling him not to do something or freaking out on him, it just rolls off him, and he does exactly what he wants anyway.

He steamrolls me in a way that doesn't feel like steamrolling at all. It feels a little like...letting someone else carry the load for once. It's been a long time since I've done that. I've been so hellbent on trying to prove to Nash that I can take care of myself that I've forced myself to carry everything alone.

Noah doesn't ask if he can help carry some of the load. He just does it. Even when I argue about it, he does it. That's dangerous. I could get addicted to it. Just like I could get addicted to the way he calls me baby.

I like it way more than I should.

"I'm going to pack," I grumble.

This time, I make it two steps before Noah stops me. Only, he doesn't halt me with words. He stops me with his hand on my arm.

"Dimples."

I'm not sure if it's his closeness, the last few hours, the lack of sleep, the fact that I've had a crush on him for years, or temporary insanity, but as soon as I feel his hand on my arm, the ability to think rationally vanishes in a puff of smoke. I practically launch myself at him, desperate to feel his lips against mine again.

"Fuck," he grunts, knocked back a step. His arms lash around me, dragging me up against the hard wall of his chest. His lips come down over mine, sending a wave of heat surging through me.

All the back and forth and worries and fear and doubts fall silent as pure bliss courses through my veins. It ignites my bloodstream, pouring molten desire straight into the very heart of me. I gasp against his lips, shaken to my very foundation by the intensity of his kiss and my reaction to it. By how desperately I don't want it to end. And by one simple truth...this man will consume me if I let him.

Chapter Six

Noah

Aspen wraps herself around me, kissing me as if she needs me more than she needs air. I thrust my hand into her hair, anchoring her to me as I lick into her mouth to get another taste of her. She's the sweetest little caramel morsel, far more addictive than the coffee she serves up or the scones she bakes to perfection.

I run my free hand down her back to her round ass. She whimpers when I squeeze one plump cheek in my hand, testing the weight of it. I want to smack it to watch it bounce and jiggle. I already know it will. Christ, I want to see it when it does. Preferably with her stretched out over my lap, moaning my name.

Her teeth sink into my bottom lip, delivering an impatient, impertinent little bite.

My dick imprints itself against my zipper.

I growl, boosting her up into my arms. Packing her shit can wait. I need to know what this goddess sounds like when she's coming all over my tongue. Right fucking now.

"Where's your room, Dimples?"

"Hall," she gasps, wrapping her legs around my waist. Her hands delve into my hair.

I plant both hands on her ass, charging down the hall with her. The first door we pass is a bathroom. The second is a small office. The third is her bedroom. It's not much bigger than the office, but it's calm and comforting.

I kick the door closed to keep Brick out and then march toward the bed. Fluffy throw pillows land in a heap on the floor as I drop her in the middle of the bed. She cries out, startled. Before the sound even dies, I'm on her again, taking her lips in another deep kiss.

Jesus. I can't stop kissing her.

"I want to taste you. Tell me I can." I break away from her lips, leaving a trail of kisses down her throat.

"I...I..."

"You need to come, baby. I can feel it."

"I've never..." Her soft whisper barely reaches me.

I lift my head, meeting her gaze. "Me either."

She blinks those long lashes at me, shock painted across her gorgeous face. "You're a virgin?"

"Is that so hard to believe?"

"Yes."

I chuckle at her response. "There's a reason your brother trusted me with you, Dimples."

"He knows?"

"It's not a secret." I brush my thumb across her bottom lip, trying not to bite it. Focusing on this conversation when she's beneath me is damn hard. "I've never hidden who I am from the people who matter." I pause. "You're one of those people, in case you're wondering."

Her gaze flits across my face, searching for something. Some hint that I'm just fucking with her, perhaps. She doesn't trust easily. I think she wants to trust me, though. I see it in her eyes. But she's afraid to take that leap. Afraid, perhaps, of where she might land.

I get it. Putting your heart in someone else's hands is a terrifying prospect. I think maybe it's the most terrifying prospect for a woman like Aspen, one so fiercely independent that she moved across the country alone just to put space between her and her overprotective brother. She's never been in love before, but she has known loss. An infinite well of it. How daunting it must seem to risk her heart knowing how badly it can break.

But Aspen is no coward. She doesn't run from the things that frighten her. When faced with a choice between doing what's safe and doing what scares her, I think she'd choose what scares her every single time.

Trusting me scares the hell out of her.

"Kiss me," she whispers.

I willingly oblige, brushing my lips across hers until she softens beneath me, going pliant in my arms with a sweet sigh of surrender. Tension drains from her, her fears lying quietly.

I kiss her until she's shifting restlessly beneath me, little whimpers breaking from her lips. She needs release. I know she didn't sleep any better than I did last night. Nearly being shot this morning didn't help. She needs five minutes to forget everything but how good she can feel.

Maybe it's selfish of me to want to be the one who gives her that, but I fucking need it. I'm losing it for her. In more ways than one.

Little by little, she's consuming me. Every thought leads back to her. Obsession has taken root over the last twenty-four hours, and it's only growing stronger.

I've been certain of exactly two things in my life. Hockey and the woman beneath me. She feels like my future, deep in my bones. I can't explain it. Hell, I'm not sure there is an explanation that doesn't sound completely insane. But I saw her, and I knew. Just like that.

I need her on the same page. By any means necessary.

I kiss my way down her throat, pulling her shirt up at the same time. There's no way I'm getting a taste of her without seeing her spread out beneath me.

She shivers as I skim my hands up her sides, loving her softness. Her skin. Her body. All of it is soft and perfect.

My dick has never been this hard. I've never wanted to get inside someone as badly as I want in her.

Hanging onto my virginity was never the battle people seem to think it was. I didn't dodge temptation at every turn. No one ever interested me enough to tempt my focus away from my career. Not until now. Not until her.

She leans up, allowing me to pull her shirt off over her head. I drop it off the side of the bed, laying her back to get a look at her.

Early morning sunlight spills in through windows, giving her a golden glow. Her full breasts peek from the tops of her red bra. Her hard nipples press against the thin fabric. She's so goddamn beautiful.

"Jesus, Dimples," I whisper, running my thumb over her nipple. "I didn't know you were going to blow my mind before I ever got my mouth on you."

A pretty blush climbs up her cheeks. Her eyes flit across my face, searching again. Whatever she sees there makes her smile. "I always thought supermodels would be more your type."

"Fuck no." I grimace at the thought, not because I have anything against supermodels but simply because the thought is preposterous to me. And then her statement truly sinks in. "You thought about me."

"No!"

"You did."

"Maybe a little," she confesses in a whisper.

"How much is a little?"

"You were my first crush." She looks up at me through her lashes. "Maybe you still are."

I growl, leaning down over her again. My teeth close around her nipple.

"Noah!"

I chuckle against her breast. "I like the thought of you thinking about me, Dimples. A whole helluva lot."

She moans my name, pulling my hair as I suck and bite her nipples through her bra. I slide my hand down her round belly, aiming for heaven.

She doesn't stop me. Instead, her legs fall open as if in invitation.

I take it, cupping her pussy through her pants.

"Noah," she moans.

"I can already feel how wet you are, Aspen." I press my face to her throat, trying like hell not to come in my pants here and now. "You're fucking soaked for me."

"Yes. Please, Noah."

I groan, her sweet little plea driving me closer to the edge. I need to get her off fast. If I don't, there's no way I'm going to keep my dick out of her.

I quickly undo her pants, working them down her legs. She helps by kicking her shoes off. Together, we manage to slip her pants off, leaving them dangling from the side of the bed.

"Jesus," I groan, though I think it might be a prayer of gratitude. Because Aspen in nothing but a bra and panties is a sight to behold. I stare at her for a long moment, trying to burn this vision into my brain.

"You're making me nervous."

"You're making me forget that I'm supposed to be a gentleman," I return.

She tilts her head as if she isn't sure what I mean.

"You've got my cock so hard I can't think straight," I clarify.

"Oh. Then don't think."

"Don't tempt me, baby. I'll be fucking my kid into you faster than you can say my name."

I don't know if she takes that as a challenge, if she's trying to push me over the edge, if she just enjoys torturing me, or if she just can't help herself, but mischief flashes in her eyes. She meets my gaze. "Noah," she says, smirking.

I launch myself at her, falling on her like a man possessed. She gasps as my lips glide down her abdomen, paying homage to the little stretch marks that I find so fucking sexy. She may be twelve years younger than me, but she's all woman, in every way.

Her hands delve into my hair again, fingers plucking at the short strands. I nip her lower belly, prying her legs farther apart.

Cum spills into my boxers in a steady stream as her intoxicating scent hits me. I bury my face in her pussy, breathing her in. Even here, she smells like peaches and caramel.

I press my tongue to the seam of her panties, tasting her through them. That little taste annihilates my self-control as soon as it hits my tongue.

Ah, fuck.

I yank her panties to the side, using my tongue to part her folds on my way to her clit.

"Noah!" Her shout rings out around us, her body jolting.

I eat her like a starving man, gorging myself on her as she shouts and shakes and cries out for me. Her juices drench my face as I drag her closer, closer, until there's nowhere else for her to go except for on my tongue.

She claws my shoulders when I force the tip inside her tight little hole to fuck her with it. Her sobs grow louder.

She's going to come.

I grind my nose against her clit and stiffen my tongue, forcing it deeper.

Her body seizes up. My name leaves her lips in a euphoric cry, and she shatters, soaking my face.

I eat her through it, and then clean up the mess I made.

She falls limp beneath me, breathing hard. Her auburn hair is tangled around her flushed face. Her lips swollen from my kisses. Her expression soft.

"Beautiful," I whisper, crawling up her body to pull her into my arms.

CHAPTER SEVEN

Aspen

"Aspen."

I jolt awake, crying out in shock as someone shakes me. A man looms over me. For a moment, I think it's one of the men from the shop. And then I see familiar green eyes, and a wave of relief hits me.

"Noah," I croak. Why is my throat so dry?

"Are you okay, Dimples?"

"I..." I stare at him blankly, trying to take stock. Everything is fuzzy and muted, like I'm still half asleep. "I was having a nightmare."

"Yeah," he mutters, his tone grim. "A bad one from the way it sounded." He perches on the side of the bed beside me, reaching out. I flinch without meaning to do it. He notices but doesn't say anything. He simply pauses for a moment to give me time to adjust and then slowly continues moving his hand toward me to brush hair out of my face. "Want to talk about it?"

I try to remember details, but they're hazy. "I think I was dreaming about what happened at the shop," I say through a yawn. "I remember someone chasing me with a gun."

"Jesus."

"I should probably talk to someone," I sigh.

"Probably," he agrees.

"I did after the accident." I'm not sure why I tell him this.

"Yeah?"

I nod, dragging myself into a sitting position and then draping the sheet up with me to cover myself. Being the only one mostly naked feels a little too exposed right now. "I had nightmares for a long time afterward. Nash thought therapy might help, so I saw a shrink twice a week for the first year to try to work through everything, and then once a month until I was like sixteen."

"Did it help?"

"I guess so." I rub sleep from my eyes and sigh again. "I stopped reliving the accident every night, at least. What time is it?"

"It's a little after noon."

I blink twice. "I've been asleep for four hours?"

"You needed it. You had a shit morning."

I laugh abruptly. "That's one way to put it."

Noah cracks a smile.

"Did you sleep?"

"A little," he says. "The sheriff brought over some photos for you to look at. And I had to make some calls."

"Practice!" I cry. "You had practice this morning."

"It's cool, Dimples. I let Coach know what was going on. He's not stressing about me missing one practice." He grimaces. "We do have to bus out for a game the day after tomorrow, though. It's in Oklahoma."

"So you'll go to your game, and I'll stay here," I say.

His brows furrow. "I already talked to Jack. If the sheriff hasn't caught the fuckers who broke into the shop by then, we're going to hire a bodyguard for you until I get back."

"You're...what?" I splutter, certain I heard him wrong.

"It won't be permanent, baby. Only while I'm gone," he says, confirming that I didn't mishear him at all. The crazy man actually wants to hire a bodyguard.

"Are you insane?" I press my hands to my overheated cheeks, and the sheet slips.

To his credit, his gaze only drifts to my boobs for a brief second before returning to my face. "Someone tried to shoot you this morning, Aspen. Had his aim been better, he would have shot you."

"I'm aware. I was there," I remind him. "I'm the one who had to flee for my life. But hiring a bodyguard is taking this to an extreme."

"They'll sit outside," he says, trying to convince me. "I'd feel a helluva lot better leaving if I know you're not completely on your own while I'm out of town."

"Before we get carried away, can I at least see the photos Dillon dropped off?" I ask, more to buy myself time to think than anything. The more he talks, the less I like the thought of being on my own right now, and I'm not sure I really like how that feels. I've never been afraid in my own home before. I don't want to be afraid now, either.

"Shit. Yeah." He hops up from the side of the bed. "I'll go get them."

"Wait!"

He turns to look at me.

"Um, just give me a minute, and I'll come look," I mumble, not really wanting to look at them in here. This room is my sanctuary. Maybe it's silly, but I don't want to pollute it with bad memories or painful things.

Noah's expression softens as if he understands. Maybe he does. It's overwhelming how easily he sees through me. It doesn't feel as if I've known him a day. It feels as if he's been part of my life for so much longer than that. There's a sense of...fatalism, perhaps. As if we aren't learning one another for the first time, but simply relearning one another.

It's disconcerting and thrilling at the same time.

"I'll wait in the kitchen," he says, ducking out of the room.

I flop backward on the bed, pulling a pillow over my face. I don't know what happened to my life in the last twenty-four hours, but it's become a strange, strange place. And I don't entirely hate it. "You've lost your mind," I mutter to myself, tossing the pillow aside and rolling off the side of the bed. I quickly shimmy into my clothes and then scurry to the bathroom.

The woman staring back at me in the mirror doesn't even look familiar. I'm not put together or composed. My hair is a tangled mess. My lips are swollen. There's a look in my eyes I've never seen before now. It's...happiness.

Ah, crap. I'm falling in love with him.

Hard.

It's the only explanation for the buoyant feeling bubbling up from deep in my chest. Even though I should be afraid and angry, I'm not. I'm overwhelmed. I'm anxious. I don't want a bodyguard. But I'm not mad at Noah for being concerned enough to think I need one. I just...part of me can't help but wonder if he's doing it because he cares or if it's doing it because Nash would expect it.

Ask him, a little voice whispers.

I meet my gaze in the mirror, resolving to do just that. It's better to know than to keep spinning in circles, right? My stomach quivers with nerves.

I splash water on my face, brush my teeth, and then run a comb through my hair, trying to tame it. When it still doesn't lay right, I give up and scrape it into a messy bun before heading toward the kitchen to look at the photos Dillon sent over.

Noah's leaning against the counter with Brick in his arms. My cat is purring so loud, I hear him from halfway across the room. He looks perfectly content with Noah scratching his ears.

"He likes you," I murmur.

"Surprised?"

"Yes."

Noah grins.

"I mean, he doesn't like most people. He usually hides when people come over." The last time Nash visited, Brick bit him when he tried to pick him up. In Brick's defense, I'd probably bite my brother, too.

"We have an understanding."

"You have an understanding with my cat," I repeat, amused.

"Mmhmm." Noah's grin widens. "He's going to help me keep an eye on you. In exchange, I'm going to feed him extra when you aren't looking."

"Noah!" I shake my head, laughing. "He's on a diet."

"Calories don't count at my house, Dimples."

"Are we still going to your house?"

"Unless you're ready to share a room with me."

I hesitate for a moment. Am I ready?

"Can I ask you a question? And I need you to be honest with me," I say, wrapping my arms around myself as I lean against the small two-seater table.

"I won't lie to you."

"Why are you here?"

He eyes me levelly.

"I mean, if you're just here because Nash asked you to look after me, you don't have to act like this is more than that, Noah. It won't hurt my feelings. But I'd rather know now than after..."

"After what?"

"Nothing," I mumble. "I'd just rather know now."

He leans down, gently placing Brick on the floor. As he straightens, his gaze locks on mine, and my mouth goes dry. That look in his eyes... Lord. It pierces right through me, making my knees weak.

He paces toward me, moving like a leopard on the prowl.

"You think I'm here because of Nash, Aspen?"

"I don't..." I lick my lips. Now that I've said it out loud, it sounds crazy. "I don't know."

"He asked me to keep an eye on you, but he isn't the reason my fucking heart stopped beating when you called me this morning." He takes another step toward me and then another. "He isn't the reason I didn't sleep last night." Another step. "He isn't the reason I can still taste you on my tongue." He stops in front of me, still holding my gaze.

"And he damn sure isn't going to be the reason I put a ring on your finger as soon as you let me."

"I..." I swallow hard, rendered speechless, perhaps for the first time in my life.

"I'm exactly where I want to be, protecting the one thing in this town that matters." He slides his hand around the back of my neck, pulling me into him. His lips brush my forehead. "And I'm not going anywhere, so you might as well get used to it now."

Well, I guess that's clear enough, isn't it?

"**H**ere," he says a few minutes later, dropping a photo album in front of me. "These are the photos the sheriff wants you to look through."

"Dillon."

"What?"

"His name is Dillon. He isn't the kind of sheriff who likes to be called *the sheriff*." I stare at the photo album. It's a nondescript black, and a lot thicker than I thought it would be. "I thought he was just sending a couple of photos."

"He wants you to go through all the photos he's got of people matching the descriptions you gave him," Noah says. "And what kind of sheriff doesn't like to be called sheriff?"

"Dillon," I answer, flipping open the album. I'm not sure what I expected, but it's just photos. Most of them aren't even mugshots. They're five-by-eight images of men against plain blue backgrounds. I flip through several pages, surprised at how many of them are familiar.

"You know most of the men in town, Dimples?"

"Most of the ones who come into the shop regularly."

He grunts...whatever that means. "You have a lot of men coming in?"

"Sometimes." I flip to the next page, examining those photos. Neither of them is the guys from the shop, either. I think one of them might be the mayor's brother, though. He looks like the mayor, anyway. "Why?"

"No reason," Noah mutters.

I bite my lip, fighting a smile. Is he jealous? "Are you worried you have competition?"

"There is no competition. You're mine," he growls.

He's right. There is no competition. I've never even considered dating any of the men who have asked me out at the shop. I simply wasn't interested. Noah, though? He's in a category all on his own.

"Maybe I'll spend some time at the shop when you go back to work. Make sure no one is fucking with you."

I can't fight my smile this time. I turn to look at him over my shoulder. "You're crazy, you know that, right?"

He narrows his eyes at me. "Look through the photos, Dimples. We have shit to do."

I laugh quietly and turn back to the photo album, flipping through the pages. Halfway through, I stop flipping suddenly. My hands tremble as I point at the image.

"Him," I say. "This is the guy who had the gun." He has blue eyes. They're like ice as he glares at the camera, his jaw set. His hair is a pale red. The freckles scattered across his face stand in testament to his age, but he's...hard in a way that belies it, as if he's seen too much.

"You're sure?" Noah asks, placing his hand on the back of my chair as he leans down to get a better look at the photo.

"I'm positive." I couldn't forget him even if I wanted to forget. I guess it comes with the territory when someone tries to shoot you. You remember them, even if you don't want to remember, as if their image is imprinted on your psyche.

Noah pulls out his phone and snaps a photo of the image. I think he's sending it to Dillon, but I don't ask. I flip to the next page. Now that I've found the one guy, I want to find the other. I flip through page after page of images but don't come across his photo.

I flip the book closed with a disappointed huff. "I hoped they'd both be in there," I admit.

"The odds of that happening weren't great. But at least the sheriff—Dillon—knows where to start now."

"Did he say if that's the guy Jack thinks it is?" I ask.

"Yeah. It's him."

I don't know why, but I'd kind of hoped it wasn't. Maybe because I wanted it to be someone less dangerous, perhaps. As if anyone willing to shoot at an innocent person isn't dangerous. But this guy, Silar, has been in prison. He invaded someone's home at gunpoint with them inside. That's dangerous to the nth degree.

He's the kind of person who would come back to finish the job if he knew I got a good look at him and could identify him. That's a sobering thought. Maybe Noah isn't overreacting by suggesting a bodyguard. Maybe I've been underreacting.

"Do you really think a bodyguard is necessary?" I ask quietly.

"I don't know," he says after a moment, "but I'd rather have someone outside while I'm gone than risk it. I'm already going to be hearing that fucking gunshot in my nightmares for the rest of my life."

"Okay," I say, giving in. "Then I guess that's what we'll do."

"Yeah?"

"Yeah," I sigh. If it makes him feel better, I can't say no. I'm no longer sure I even want to say no anyway. "But can I ask for one favor?"

"Name it."

"Can it please be Giant, um, Cormac Carmichael?"

"Yeah. Fuck, yeah, Dimples."

I exhale a relieved breath. At least it'll be someone I know and trust.

CHAPTER EIGHT

Noah

"Why isn't my sister answering my calls?" Nash demands as soon as I answer the phone.

"Maybe because she's busy?" I suggest, lying my ass off. She's not busy. She's curled up on the couch beside me right now, watching some fucking Lifetime movie about a pregnant girl and her new boyfriend or something. I don't know. I stopped paying attention half an hour ago.

"How do you know? Are you with her right now?"

"Maybe."

Nash curses under his breath. "It's ten o'clock at night, Diamante."

"We're watching a movie."

"Where?"

"At my place."

"I'm regretting giving you permission to get to know her," he mutters. "You're already moving too goddamn fast for me."

"Good thing it's not your business then, huh?"

He curses again. "Let me talk to my sister before I decide I don't like you."

I chuckle and hold the phone out to Aspen. "Your brother wants to talk to you, Dimples. He's cranky."

Aspen groans before plucking the phone from my hand. "What do you want now?" she says, exasperated. I don't know what he says, but she huffs and then smiles. "If I say no, are you going to fire him from babysitting duty?"

"He can't fire me, baby. I already quit."

I think he hears me because she listens for a minute and then laughs. "He said quitting is for vaginas."

"He would know, considering he is one."

"He says he heard that," she says, smiling from ear to ear.

"He was supposed to hear it." I climb to my feet, pressing a kiss to her forehead. "I'm going to check on Brick while you talk to your brother."

"Okay," she whispers, staring up at me with a soft expression, happiness shining in her eyes. I like that look on her face a helluva lot better than I like seeing her afraid and crying, that's for sure.

I duck out of the room in search of Brick, smiling when I hear her tell Nash to mind his own business and stop trying to be the boss of her and her cat. She's so fucking sassy. It shouldn't make my dick nearly as hard as it does. And yet, I love it. I don't know many people who would bounce back from the morning she had as fast as she has, but she just deals with it, refusing to let it slow her down. I know that doesn't mean she's over it. Of fucking course she's not over it. But she's coping, and that's a good sign.

Brick is sprawled across the very center of the pool table in my game room, passed out. Which is pretty much where we left him a few hours ago. He explored for a while when we got here, and then decided he preferred this room. I don't blame him. All the cool shit is in here.

Aspen's favorite room is the kitchen. I didn't even have to ask to know. She lit up as soon as she set eyes on it. I can't fucking wait to see her in it, putting it to use. I have a feeling it's her happy place, the one place where she feels most connected to her parents and where she came from.

I pour a little food into Brick's bowl—either he's dead to the world or simply not hungry because he barely even twitches—and then head down the hall to grab Aspen's phone from the bedroom. She tried to put it in the guest room, but I want her in my space. If she's not ready for me to be in there with her, I won't rush her. But I want her scent all over my pillows when she leaves. Knowing she's in my bed is the only damn way I'm going to get any sleep.

I grab the phone and jog back to the living room. She's curled up on the couch again, watching her movie. She tilts her head back, smiling when she sees me. "Hey."

"How's Nash?" I drop her phone in her lap.

"Bossy." She rolls her eyes, but she can't hide the little smile on her face. Her brother may drive her crazy, but I don't think she'd change anything about him. It's obvious she adores him. I think she's just tired of being smothered. She isn't the type of woman meant to be kept in a cage or loomed over. The allure of freedom and independence is too strong. "He said he'll call you tomorrow."

"What did he want?"

"To complain that I haven't answered my phone all day." She grimaces. "He worries more than he should."

I slide onto the couch beside her, not saying anything. After this morning, I think he has every reason to worry. But he doesn't know what happened yet. He's going to be mad as hell when he finds out I kept it from him. I'll cross that bridge when I come to it. The important thing is that she's safe and she'll remain safe. I won't fail on that front.

"He worries because he loves you." I brush hair off her face. "That's not wrong, is it?"

"No," she sighs quietly. "But he's worried about me for long enough. He gave up half of his life to raise me. When does he stop worrying long enough to live the rest of it?" Her eyes meet mine, wide and earnest. "That's why I moved here. Because he was never going to stop being my parent and learn to be Nash so long as I was there."

I process this for a moment. She isn't angry at him. She feels guilty, as if raising her was a burden on him. One that he's continued to carry well past the time he should have. I don't think Nash sees it the same way. In fact, I know he doesn't.

"He didn't give anything up to raise you, Dimples."

"He did." She turns to face me. "You know he was supposed to enter the draft right after the accident? But I was in the hospital, so he skipped it. When he went to training camp the following year, he wasn't selected for a team. It took an entire year after that before he finally got a contract. That's how he landed on the Yellowjackets and then got called up to the Capitals. He would have been in the NHL a lot earlier if it hadn't been for me."

"He made the choice he could live with, Aspen," I say quietly. "I know your brother. Hockey is just a game. For most guys, playing for the NHL is just a dream. If we're lucky, we get to live that dream for a while. But it's still just a dream, a goal on a list. Family, though? That's forever. If he had to do it again, he'd do the exact same thing and have no regrets. He has none now."

"That doesn't mean he shouldn't get to live his own life. So long as I was there, he would have kept spending all of his time with me and none of it doing the things he should be doing."

"What are you hiding from him?" I watch her face, searching for an answer. "What are you trying so hard to keep him from finding out?"

"That I'm buying the coffee shop," she whispers. "I'll have enough money to buy half of it from Jack at the end of the month."

"You think Nash will try to stop you," I guess.

"I think…" She pauses, dragging the tip of her tongue over her bottom lip. "I *know* that once he realizes that I'm here permanently, he's going to lose his mind. He'll try to give up hockey to move here or something crazy. I'm trying to keep that from happening for as long as I can."

"You don't want him here?"

"I don't want him giving up something he loves because he thinks I need him to save me," she clarifies with a shake of her head. "I don't want him to sacrifice anything else for me. I want him to live his dreams. I owe him that." Tears well in her eyes. "I'm terrified he'll give it all up to follow me here just because he doesn't want to let me go. I almost died, and it changed him. I think it *broke* him."

Jesus. She's not fighting so hard for her independence. She's fighting so hard for his. In her eyes, he sacrificed everything to raise her, and he's been sacrificing every day since. She doesn't want to be the reason he lives with regret. She wants him to heal.

"Come here." I drag her across the couch onto my lap, holding her close. "You need to talk to him about how you feel, baby. He isn't unreasonable. Just worried."

"Maybe," she whispers, laying her head on my shoulder. The doubt in her voice makes her sound so much smaller than she is, so much more vulnerable than the fierce woman who has been giving me hell since I walked into the coffee shop yesterday morning.

I make an instant decision.

"Are you into this movie?"

"Not really. I just think the actor is kind of hot."

I growl, nipping her ear. "You want to try that again?"

"No? I'm pretty sure I said what I meant the first time."

I secure her against me and climb to my feet, making her laugh and cling to my shoulders.

"I was just kidding, Noah!" she cries.

"Too late." I palm her ass, marching toward the bedroom.

"Fine, I meant it anyway," she mutters, making me smile. She doesn't give an inch, and I fucking love it. Nothing makes me hotter than her mouth and the shit that comes out of it.

I deposit her on her feet at the foot of the bed, tipping my face down to take her mouth in a hard kiss. "Go get ready for bed before I decide not to let you sleep at all."

She ducks under my arm, scurrying toward the bathroom. Halfway there, she pauses, glancing over her shoulder at me. "Hey, Noah?"

"Yeah, Dimples?"

"You're hotter."

Fuck. I take a step toward her.

She squeaks and runs toward the bathroom, closing the door between us.

"Quit fidgeting."

"I'm not," she lies, rolling onto her back even as she says it.

I smile up at the ceiling. She hasn't been able to settle since her ass landed in the bed half an hour ago. She's on the far side of the bed, an ocean of empty sheets between us, but I can feel the tension radiating from her all the way over here. She's thinking about me eating her earlier today.

"You scared you're going to moan my name in your sleep, baby?"

"You wish."

I roll onto my side, facing her. "You did earlier today."

"I did not."

"Noah," I mimic. "Noah."

Her cold little foot crosses the great divide between us, landing against my shin. I chuckle and grab it, using it as leverage to haul her across the bed toward me.

"You messed up, Dimples," I breathe, rolling on top of her. "You should have stayed on your side of the bed if you wanted me to keep my hands to myself."

"I was on my side of the bed."

"Liar." I brush my nose against hers, dragging her leg up over my hip. "You want me to make you come again, don't you?"

"Noah."

"I'll give you whatever you want, Aspen. All you have to do is say the words."

"Say w-what?" Her eyes seek me in the dark.

"Say, 'I want you to make me come, Noah,'" I murmur, my lips a mere breath from hers.

"Noah," she whispers again, her tone pleading.

"Say it."

"Please make me come, Noah," she says, her voice shaking. "Please."

I groan, touching my lips to hers as I reach between us, seeking out her heat. She wore a tiny pair of shorts and a t-shirt to bed, but they don't offer much protection. I slip my hand beneath the band, eager to feel her slick folds against my fingers again. Eager to listen to her moaning my name while she shatters around me.

She throws her head back, moaning quietly as I part her slit with my thumb. Her clit is already hard and swollen, just begging for attention. I bet she's been thinking about this since she laid down next to me. God knows I have. My dick hasn't gone down since she walked out of the bathroom.

I run my thumb in circles around her clit, licking and kissing all over her neck at the same time. Her nails scrabble down my back, little puffs of sound escaping her lips. She writhes against me, rocking against my hand and pleading quietly.

"You sound so fucking good when you're begging for my cock," I groan, nipping her throat. "I can't wait until you're stretched around me. When I get in you, I'm taking you bare. There won't be anything stopping me from planting my kid in your belly."

She trembles beneath me, moaning louder.

"Everyone at the shop will know you're taken then. There won't be any hiding it." I press my lips to her ear, grinding my thumb against her clit. "They'll know I'm fucking crazy about you."

She cries out, shattering beneath me.

I press my lips to her throat, stroking her clit as she shakes her way through it, whimpering.

"That's it," I croon against her skin. "Good girl, Dimples."

"Noah," she moans.

"I love the way you say my name when you're in heaven. It's so fucking sweet." I press another kiss to her throat and then slowly pull my hands from her panties. I roll her onto my chest before popping my fingers into my mouth to lick them clean. My eyes roll back in my head, my dick pulses in my boxers.

Christ, I'm not going to survive much longer without getting inside her.

Her hand lands against my abdomen, slowly creeping downward.

I quickly grab her wrist, pulling her hand up to place a kiss on her knuckles. "Get some sleep, baby. You've had a long day."

"What about you?"

"I'm good, baby."

"But you didn't..."

"No, and I'm not going to." I tip her head back, brushing a kiss across her lips. "Not until you're ready for my babies. Now, go to sleep."

"I'll argue with you tomorrow," she mumbles, already half asleep.

I chuckle, my heart pulsing with emotion. There's no denying it. I'm in love with her. If I can't convince her that she feels the same way, she's going to rip my heart out of my chest.

Chapter Nine

Aspen

"Are you finished pouting yet?"

I turn a dark glower on Noah. "I'm not pouting. I'm annoyed. There's a difference, you know."

"If you say so." His lips twitch, letting me know he doesn't believe me.

"You and Jack aren't allowed to be friends. You're bossy enough on your own."

"You're just mad because he's on my side."

"He's only on your side because he likes your team."

Noah grins at me. "So you're big mad, huh?"

"Yes! I don't see why I can't work for two hours while you go to practice. It's not like I was alone," I complain, tossing my head back against the seat rest. "Jack is there.

There are customers. No one is going to try to shoot me in a store full of customers, Noah."

"When we tell Nash what happened, I'd like to be able to tell him that I didn't let you out of my sight until we had a bodyguard sitting outside your door, Dimples. Otherwise, he's going to be pissed that I didn't tell him immediately."

"I thought you said you weren't spying for him."

"I'm not, but this isn't something you just fail to mention."

He's right. This is major. But I'm not over the fact that Jack basically kicked me out of the shop and Noah helped. Having them on the same team is highly inconvenient for me. I can only imagine how much worse it'll be if Nash gets wind of the fact that I'm buying the shop and tries to pick up his life to move here. I'll never have a moment's p eace.

"What kind of favor do you owe my brother, anyway?" I ask Noah. He never did tell me.

"I don't owe him a favor."

"So you agreed to keep an eye on me for the fun of it?" I blink at him. "There's no way you're that bored."

He laughs quietly, rolling to a stop at the light outside the arena. "I'm not bored at all. But he's a friend and I know how important you are to him."

"Well, that's kind of a letdown," I mutter, making him laugh again. "You don't even have useful dirt on him that I can use against him later." I glance at him curiously. "Does he have any on you?"

"Nah," he says, pulling into the parking lot of the arena. "I'm very well-behaved."

"Right," I snort, not believing that for a minute. "I bet your teammates have all kinds of dirt on you." I smile at the prospect. "Huh. Being dragged here against my will is starting to look promising."

"Don't believe anything they tell you," he says, pulling into a spot at the back of the arena. There are a few other vehicles already in the lot. "Especially not the big one."

"The big one? Uh, have you looked at the roster lately? You're all big, Noah."

"I'm talking about Atlas. He's insane."

"That's basically a prerequisite for being a goalie," I remind him. Nash tells me stories about the goalies all the time. As far as I can tell, they're all crazy. I think it's because they spend so much time in the goal with nothing to do but talk to themselves.

"He's the reason I have a tattoo on my ass."

I stop in the act of unbuckling my seatbelt. "What?"

"It's a long story."

"I've got time."

"He wanted Mexican food, which he can apparently only get in actual Mexico," Noah says. "Don't ask me why because I don't know. So he dragged my ass down the

Nuevo Laredo on our first weekend off. Tequila is fucking stronger there. A lot stronger."

I burst into laughter. "Tequila is not stronger in Mexico, Noah."

"It is if you drink enough of it," he mutters. "We drank way too goddamn much of it. The next thing I know, I'm at the hotel, staring at a hockey puck tattooed on my ass."

I laugh so hard I can't breathe. Tears leak from the corners of my eyes as I try to picture him trying to figure out what happened.

"It's not funny. The damn thing says *Get Pucked*."

"No, it doesn't."

"It does."

"Stop," I wheeze, pretty sure I'm going to die if I don't breathe soon. "Oh my God. I'm telling everyone."

He growls, reaching over the console to drag me into his arms.

"I will spank your gorgeous ass if you tell a soul," he vows, but he's smiling so the threat isn't very effective. It's even less effective since I kind of like the thought of him spanking me. "You're taking that secret to the grave, baby."

"Maybe," I whisper, wrapping my arms around his neck. I pull him down toward me, eager to feel his lips against mine again. I might be addicted to his kisses. Who am I kidding? I think I'm addicted to him. He's slipped seamlessly into my life, turning it upside down and inside out.

He's changing me in ways I didn't expect. It's profound and subtle at the same time. I feel more like me than I think I ever have before. I'm less alone than I have been in two years, but I feel more in control of my future than ever. As if some part of me instinctively knows that he's what led me here. This is what I was running toward.

"Fuck," he groans, breaking the kiss. "How am I supposed to practice when you've got my dick hard as a rock?"

I press my lips to his ear, getting as close to him as possible. "Think about the tattoo on your ass," I whisper reaching for the door handle. "That should take care of the problem."

He growls and lunges for me, but I throw myself out of the truck, laughing.

N oah's teammates are chaotic good. It's the only way to describe them. They're loud and boisterous, spending as much time giving each other grief as they do actually practicing. It's fascinating to watch, though.

I haven't been to a hockey practice in a long time. Nash stopped letting me attend when he went into the AHL. He said he didn't want me growing up around a bunch of rowdy hockey players. I think he was worried that some of the younger players would try to flirt with me or something. I'm not entirely sure. Some of the youngest guys are barely out of high school. They're still just kids.

It's crazy to me to imagine living the kind of life they do at any age, let alone at eighteen or nineteen. Nash has always seemed so much older and wiser. Even though he played on a college team first, he still would have entered the draft at twenty. I don't think I ever considered how overwhelming that had to be.

I think I've always felt so much guilt over everything he gave up that I've never let myself see it from a different perspective. But as I sit on the bench, watching Noah and his teammates zip back and forth across the ice, I can't help but consider that maybe Nash didn't give up as much as I've always thought he did. Maybe he made the choice he did as much for himself as he made it for me.

"Aspen."

I turn at the sound of my voice to find Dillon squeezing his way down the bench toward me.

"Hey," I murmur, my gaze falling to the album in his hands. "More photos?"

"Just one this time." He stops beside me, looking out at the ice.

Noah must see him because he breaks away from Colter and Reid and skates in our direction.

"Have you found the fucker?" he growls, ice flying up from his skates when he stops against the boards.

"Working on it," Dillon says. "I've got a couple of leads, but I need your girl to look at another photo."

Noah jerks his helmet off. His short hair is smashed flat on top of his head and soaked with sweat. He watches intently as Dillon flips the album open and then turns it around for me to look at.

"Do you recognize the men in this photo?" he asks.

I stare at the photo for a long moment, an instant shock of recognition rushing through me. It's the two men from the shop. I think they're behind the bookstore right down from the shop. At least, it looks like the bookstore. The redheaded one, Silar, isn't looking at the camera as he runs past, but the other one looks right at it.

"I know him," I whisper, my stomach churning as I stare at his face. He's handsome, with stunning obsidian eyes and a cleft chin. "He was in the shop on Friday."

"You're sure?" Dillon asks.

I lift my gaze from the photo, looking at him. "I'm positive. He asked for my number." I thought he looked familiar in the shop, but it was dark and everything was chaotic. I didn't see him nearly as well as I saw his partner-in-crime. But there's no mistaking him in this photo. "He said his name was Troy."

A possessive, predatory growl emanates from Noah's throat.

"Troy Crevier," Dillon confirms. "Heir to Crevier Enterprises."

"Jesus fucking Christ," Noah curses. "You're kidding me."

Crevier Enterprises is one of the biggest trucking companies in the United States. Why is the heir of the company breaking into a coffee shop? I doubt he's hurting for cash. He probably owns more property than most of the men in this town.

"Why the fuck would the heir of a trucking company need to knock over a coffee shop?" Noah asks, echoing my thoughts.

"That's exactly what I plan to ask him," Dillon says, slipping the photo album off my lap. He flips it closed, tucking it under his arm. "Just as soon as I find him."

"You can't find him?" Noah's voice drops to a deep, menacing growl, far more intimidating than if he'd shouted the words.

"He's currently MIA." Dillon grimaces. "I've got people working on it. As soon as I find him, you'll know it."

"Is she safe in the meantime?" Noah demands, clearly not satisfied with this answer. "If he thinks she can identify him, he has more to lose than the other motherfucker. His entire family stands to lose something if she points the finger at him."

I shiver, wrapping my arms around myself.

Dillon doesn't say anything, which seems to be answer enough for Noah.

He rattles off a string of curses under his breath.

"I can assign someone to watch her," Dillon offers. "The alternative would be for you to send her somewhere else until the dust settles."

"I can't just leave town," I protest. "I have an entire business to run, Dillon."

"I can assign someone to sit on her," he says to Noah again.

"I've already got Cormac Carmichael on standby. He starts first thing in the morning."

"What do you mean, I can't go to work?" I ask, staring at Noah like he's grown a third head. "Jack's expecting me back at the shop. He has an entire company to run!"

"Not today he doesn't," Noah growls, shoving the rest of his stuff into his gym bag. "I've already talked to him. He agrees that you need to lay low until Dillon finds Troy."

"He agrees that I need to.... You *called* him already?"

"Before I hit the showers."

"I can't believe you called my boss. That's over the line, Noah."

"Believe it, baby." He lifts his gaze to mine. "When it comes to your safety, there isn't a line I'm not willing to cross. Your safety is *everything* to me. I'll do whatever I have to do to make sure my goddamn life doesn't flash before my eyes like it did yesterday morning when I heard you scream."

I want to be mad at him, but he makes it so hard. If he were anyone else, I'd be furious right now. But he says things like that, and my heart hears them before my head does. It leaps for joy, and I forget that I'm supposed to be mad. I forget that I'm supposed to be anything other than *his*.

"You are so lucky I lov..." I snap my mouth closed, eyes wide as I realize what I almost said. I'm in love with him. Crap. How, in God's name, did I fall for someone even more overprotective than my brother? I don't know, but here I am anyway. Head over heels for a crazy man.

"Say it," he growls, rising to his feet.

Part of me wants to refuse just because I'm stubborn and I never do what I'm told. But he's not demanding. He's pleading with me, begging me to say the words and release him from the bonds he's tied himself into to keep himself moving at my pace.

I don't refuse him. How can I?

"You are so lucky I love you," I say, my voice shaking. "Otherwise, I'd be kicking your a—"

That's as far as I get before he launches himself at me. My back lands against a row of lockers as his lips crash down on mine. He kisses me until I can't breathe, running his hands all over my body. He sets me ablaze, igniting me like a supernova.

"It's about goddamn time, Dimples," he growls against my lips.

I smile, beaming like the sun. "Take me home before I change my mind, Noah."

CHAPTER TEN

Noah

I don't remember the drive to the house. All I can think about is the woman sitting beside me. The one who just told me that she's in love with me. Fuck, I'd hoped. And prayed. But I didn't think I stood a chance in hell of hearing those words from her perfect lips anytime soon.

Being wrong has never felt so right.

She's in love with me. She's mine.

Fucking finally.

As soon as we pull into the driveway, she bounces out of the truck like a spring. I catch her on the front porch, crowding her up against the wall.

"You trying to get away from me, Dimples?"

"No. I'm trying to get you naked, Noah." She shoots me a cheeky grin. "I want to see this tattoo of yours."

I chuckle, tipping her face up to mine to kiss her. "Maybe I'll let you see it."

She hums against my lips as I press her back against the wall, pressing my dick against her belly. She trembles, moaning my name when she feels it.

"You keep making that sound, we aren't going to make it inside, Aspen."

She moans again, fucking with me this time.

I nip her bottom lip and then scoop her up into my arms. She immediately wraps her legs around my waist, planting her lips against the side of my throat. I growl, palming her ass as I fight to keep us upright and get the key into the lock at the same time.

"You're making it damn hard to concentrate over here."

"Good," she hums against my skin, dragging her teeth down the tendon in my neck.

I growl, nearly ripping the fucking door off the hinges in my haste to get her through it. It slams behind us. I pause long enough to lock it and then charge for the bedroom.

Her teeth close around the shell of my ear, delivering a stinging bite.

We fall in a tangle of arms and legs onto the bed. She isn't content to let me lead. She's eager to explore, running her hands all over me. Touching me like I've been doing to her for the last couple days.

I growl, arching upward as her hand brushes my cock through my sweats. "You're killing me."

"Yeah?" She likes knowing that. "Take them off, Noah. I want to see you."

"You first."

She shrugs and strips her shirt off over her head. I swallow hard when her bra immediately follows.

Somehow, she keeps getting even more beautiful every damn time I see her. It shouldn't be statistically possible, but she just gets more perfect. I'm so in love with her its ridiculous. I'm not ashamed of it, though. She could bring me to my knees with a crook of her finger and I'd happily kneel.

I strip down too, giving her what she wants. To see me. Her eyes eat me alive as I pull my shirt off and then drag my sweats down. She reaches out, running her hand down my abdomen toward my cock. There's no missing him. He's a hard bastard, pointing heavenward.

"Fuck," I groan, arching into her touch.

"You're beautiful," she says simply. Her other hand traces the tattoo running down my thigh. "I thought the hockey puck was the only one."

"No. It's the only one I regret," I say. "This is the one that matters."

"What is it?"

"A little piece of everywhere I've played," I murmur. "I've added something to it to represent every team I've played with."

She runs her gaze across it, looking at each individual piece of the whole. "The yellow and black flowers on the mountain," she murmurs. "That's for the Yellowjackets."

"It is."

"Why a clock face?" She cranes her neck to read the time displayed on it.

"It's nineteen minutes and three seconds."

"Why that time?"

"I started playing when I was three. I was drafted when I was nineteen." I pause. "When you let me put a ring on your finger, I'll have an hour hand." As far as I'm concerned, that'll be the crowning moment of my life, the most important team I'll ever join.

"Noah," she whispers, her expression softening.

I seize the opportunity and sit up, dragging her down beneath me. Her eyes flutter closed on a sigh of surrender as I kiss my way down her body, stripping her panties as I go. Her legs fall open, the invitation clear.

Her bare pussy peeks from between her thick thighs, making my dick throb. I swear, I'm obsessed with it. How sweet she tastes. How wet she gets. How fucking pink it is. Every time she lets me see it, I want to spend the rest of my life worshipping between her legs.

I place little kisses all over her thighs, taking my time with her. Her scent fills my lungs, drowning me in desire. If I died with my tongue between her legs, I wouldn't regret a goddamn second of it.

"Noah, please," she pleads as sweetly as ever. "I need you."

I take pity on her and toss her legs over my shoulder, licking her from top to bottom. Her taste hits my system as powerfully as ever. Jesus Christ. I could write poetry to this pussy.

She rocks her hips against me, mewling as I eat her like I've got all day. Shit, as far as I'm concerned I do. This right here is the only item on my agenda for the rest of the day. Her honey spills across my tongue in reward for my efforts.

I lick up every drop, savoring it. Worshipping her. My tongue runs in circles around her clit before I suck each juicy lip into my mouth. I release them with a pop, thrusting my tongue into her tight hole.

Her sounds grow louder as she grinds against my face, trying to get herself there. But that's my job now. And I'm nothing if not a conscientious employee. I suck her clit into my mouth, working two fingers inside of her. She's so goddamn tight around them.

"I can't wait to feel that around my cock, Dimples." I fuck her with my fingers, watching her face for a moment. She's lost to the pleasure, her head shifting back and forth on the pillow, her lips parted. Beautiful.

Her inner muscles flutter around my fingers, letting me know she's close. I curl my fingers up, stroking her G-spot in a firm motion. As soon as I do, she cries out, coming all over my face.

I eat her through it, leaving her limp and wrung out beneath me.

"That looked good," I growl, prowling up her body. I stop to pull her right nipple into my mouth, sucking on it. She arches toward me. I pop off and drag her left through my teeth.

She moans, running her hands up my back when I finally reach her lips. Her back arches as she seams her body to mine, eager to feel me against her. I thrust my tongue inside her mouth, playing with hers...letting her taste what I do.

"See how good you taste, Aspen?" I drag her bottom lip through my teeth. "You're already my favorite meal."

"Mmm," she sighs, scratching at my scalp. "I'm going for favorite everything, Noah."

"You're winning that race too," I say with a chuckle, situating myself between her legs. My dick slides through her sticky folds and my balls ache. "The first time is going to be fast," I warn her, knowing damn well I'm not going to last once I'm inside her. "I'm dying here."

"Then get inside me already," she demands, dragging her nails gently down my back. "Hurry, Noah."

I cover her mouth with mine, trying to silence her before her bossy little attitude has me fucking her into next week. This is her first time. I need to take care with her.

I press my cock against her entrance, pushing forward.

Her nails dig into my back as the head of my cock slips inside. Precum makes a mess of both of us.

"Goddamn, you're tight."

"I'm sorry," she sobs.

"I'm not. Fuck, you feel incredible." I thrust forward an inch, taking it slow. Painfully, exquisitely slow. It's the best kind of torture. I slip forward another inch, and then another. There's a slight tearing as the rest of her hymen gives way around my shaft.

She tenses slightly, her brow furrowing as if in pain, and I freeze, feeling like an asshole. How the fuck is it fair that it feels this goddamn good to me while she's hurting?

"I'm hurting you," I groan. "I'm sorry, Dimples. I'm an asshole."

"No," she says quickly, grabbing for me as if to keep me in place. "It was just a little pain." Her dazed, glossy eyes meet mine. "It's worth it, Noah. This is worth it."

I study her face, see the truth of her statement reflected in her eyes.

"Kiss me," I breathe.

She offers her lips up to me willingly, eagerly. I sink into her kiss...getting lost in her. I slip forward another inch. She doesn't tense again. She's relaxed beneath me, moaning quietly.

I thrust forward, not stopping until she's wrapped around all eight inches and writhing on my cock.

"Feels so good," she moans.

I groan her name, pressing my face to her chest as I try not to lose it here and now. As I revel in the moment and the feel of her tight cunt wrapped around me. She's an enchantress, pulling me deeper and deeper under her spell with every breath she takes.

"Make love to me, Noah," she pleads quietly.

Who the hell am I to tell a goddess no?

I wrap myself around her, sheltering her with my body as I slip out almost all the way and then thrust forward again. I don't take it slow this time. I drive my hips into hers, sinking eight deep.

She cries out in bliss.

I hook her legs around my waist and flip us, placing her on top, her legs splayed around my hips.

"Ride me, Dimples," I demand, wrapping my hands around her waist to help guide her. We work out the rhythm together, move together. I thrust upward every time she sinks down. She rolls her hips, grinding the root of my cock against her clit. Pushing me deeper.

Her gorgeous tits bounce with every thrust, giving me a show. It's the best damn one I've ever seen.

"You're s-so deep," she gasps, riding me harder. Faster. She throws her head back, lost in the rhythm now. She learns quick and moves like a siren, sinuous and free. "Please. Oh, please."

"What do you need, baby? Tell me, and it's yours."

"What you promised."

For a minute, I don't understand what she means, and then realization dawns. She's asking me to breed her. Ah, fuck.

My hands tighten around her waist. I take control, lifting and dropping her on my cock over and over. "Is this what you want, baby? You want me to fuck my kid into you?"

"Yes!" Her soft body undulates on top of me as she rides me, caught in a web of ecstasy. It pulls tight around us, capturing us both. Binding us together. Heart to heart. Soul to soul.

I drop her on my cock over and over, listening to her sobs grow louder. They fill the room like some carnal song only we know. One meant for our ears alone. This is us stripped to our foundation, exposed and raw.

It's messy and wild, but it's beautiful too. This is what I waited for. This moment. This woman. This is everything.

"I love you, Aspen."

She sobs, her nails digging into my thighs as she shatters around me. The power of her orgasm rips mine from me. I groan her name, spilling into her in heavy pulses that steal the breath from my lungs. It's heaven. Jesus, everything about being in her is heaven.

She grinds against me, milking my cock of every single drop, and then she falls forward, exhausted. I catch her, dragging her down to my chest. Her sweet sigh dances across my skin, hitting me right in the heart.

"I love you," I whisper again, just to make sure she knows I didn't say it in the heat of the moment. I meant that shit. With every fiber of my being.

"I love you, Noah."

Chapter Eleven

Aspen

"**N**oah, you've only been gone for fifteen minutes," I say, smiling from ear to ear as soon as I answer his call. "I told you that I'll be fine. Giant's already here."

"I know, but I forgot to tell you something."

"What?"

"I love you."

My heart turns a flip. "You told me," I whisper. Hearing him say it last night will be a memory I cherish forever. He said it again before he left this morning.

It's fast and crazy, and I don't care anymore. I don't even feel like the same person I was the day he walked into The Golden Mug. That person was terrified to trust or let people in. She thought she had to conquer the world alone. This one can't even fathom how sad that is.

I've been so afraid that nearly losing me broke something in Nash that I never realized that it broke part of me, too. I thought I was healed when the nightmares stopped, but that was wrong. One part of me never healed completely.

Nash isn't the only one who stopped living. I did, too. I've just been going through the motions ever since. Not anymore. My heart is open, and it's full.

"I know, but I thought you deserved to hear it again."

"I love you too, Noah," I murmur.

"Fuck," he groans. "Why can't this damn game be here?"

"Because the last one was."

"Smartass."

I smile. "It's one night. Brick and I will keep the bed warm for you."

"What's my boy doing?"

"Your boy? Did you just claim my cat?"

"He's our cat now, Dimples. Hate to break it to you, but I've been bribing him to the Darkside since I met him."

"Noah!" I cry, curling up on the couch. "You have to stop feeding him so much. He's on a diet."

He makes a static sound. "What's that? I can't hear you."

"I'm so telling the vet that you're overfeeding him," I vow through laughter.

"Snitches get spankings, Dimples."

"That's not how that saying goes."

"It is now."

Someone says something in the background and Noah curses. "I gotta go, baby. Coach wants us on the ice to warm up before we load up the bus."

"Okay. I'll see you tomorrow night."

"I'll call you later. Behave."

He disconnects before I can tell him that I do what I want. I fidget with my phone for a minute before dialing Nash's number.

"Aspen?" He sounds groggy. "Is everything okay?"

"Crap. I forgot how early it still is," I say apologetically. He's two hours behind me. It's not even five in the morning there. "I'll call you back later."

"It's fine. I'm up, baby sis. What's going on? Shouldn't you be elbow deep in pastry dough right now?"

"I'm taking a few days off."

"Really?"

"You don't have to sound so surprised."

"You love your job. You never take time off unless you're sick or you're flying out to visit."

"I do so take time off," I protest.

"Liar."

Brick lifts his head to glare at me, almost as if agreeing with Nash.

"Whatever," I mumble to both of them.

"You're at Noah's again."

How does he possibly know that?

"How do you possibly know that?" A frown tugs at my lips. "Did Noah tell you?"

"No, you just told me." Nash sighs heavily. "You spent the night with him."

"Maybe," I whisper.

He's quiet for a long moment and then he sighs again. "At least you picked someone worth a damn. Is he being good to you?"

"Very." I lick my lips. "He's the reason I'm calling, actually."

"You're in love with him," Nash says, not sounding surprised.

"Yes."

"I don't even have to ask to know how he feels. Knew this was coming when he told me he wasn't going to spy on you."

"That's why I'm calling."

"I won't apologize for being worried about you. You're up to something. I've known you for your entire life."

"Why did you skip the draft after the accident?"

"What?"

"Why did you skip the draft? You could have gone into the NHL that year, but you gave up your spot. It almost derailed your career," I remind him.

"You think it's your fault," he says quietly.

"I don't know," I whisper.

"I skipped the draft because I wasn't ready, Aspen. I won't say you didn't factor into my decision because you did, but you weren't the biggest part of it. We'd just lost Mom and Dad. Every damn time I was on the ice, I thought about how the accident was my fault."

"Nash." My heart sinks, tears springing to my eyes. "How can you possibly think that?"

"You don't remember, do you?" He seems surprised. "You guys were on the way to see me, Aspen. I knew it was the last game of my college career, and I wanted you guys there. Mom and Dad closed the bakeries and checked you out of school to drive down for the game."

"Nash, that doesn't make it your fault. You aren't the reason the brakes failed." Tears stream down my cheeks, my heart hurting for him. He's carried this for so long. God, no wonder he's so overprotective. He thinks he's the reason I almost died.

"I know," he says quietly. "Logically, I know that. But back then? It's all I thought about every time I hit the ice. That's why I skipped the draft. I would have washed out my first year had I gone through with it."

"I always thought you skipped it because of me." I dab at my eyes.

"It wasn't you, Aspen. Why are you asking this now? What's on your mind?"

"I'm buying the coffee shop, Nash," I confess. "And I don't want you to give up hockey to come chasing after me. My future is here, but yours has always been on the ice."

"You don't want me there." He can't hide the hurt in his voice.

"It's not about me. It's about you. You've spent the last twelve years looking after me. It's beyond time for you to have a life of your own." I expel a breath. "This is where I belong. It's where I'm happy. And I'm in his hands here."

"You mean Noah's hands."

"Yes," I acknowledge with a small smile. "But not just Noah. Jack is here, looking out for me. The sheriff is looking out for me. My friends and their husband's look out for me. This is my home now." The people here will never replace Nash in my heart. They'll never replace our parents. But they've become family too.

"This is really what you want?"

"It is," I say, my voice clear and firm.

Nash expels a heavy breath. "Okay."

"Okay? Just like that?" I ask, highly suspicious.

My brother chuckles. "I know you, baby sis. I know when you've made your mind up about something. This time, you actually believe what you're telling me. You aren't just saying it like you have been for the past two years."

"I have not just been saying it."

"Yeah, you have. Because in your heart, you knew you were there for the wrong reasons. You weren't fighting to stay for you. You were fighting to stay because you didn't think there was a better choice, or not one you were willing to live with, anyway," he says. "Now, you're fighting for you."

"My future is here."

"I'm getting that." He pauses. "Am I at least allowed to come visit?"

"Yes." I bite my lip. "But not until the end of the month."

"Why the fuck not?"

"Because that's when I sign the papers for half the shop," I say. "And if you come before then, you might not be so willing to let me stay."

"I just agreed, didn't I?"

"Yeah, but that was before I told you that Noah has a bodyguard stationed outside right now because I walked in on a robbery the other night and someone shot at me."

"What the fuck?" Nash shouts.

"See? I told you."

"Someone tried to *shoot* you?"

I cringe. Brick cringes. I think the actual house cringes. He's big mad.

"They missed, and Noah hasn't let me out of his sight since," I hurry to say. "I've already identified the two men responsible. Dillon is working on getting them brought in."

"I'm flying out."

"Don't you dare!" I shout.

"Someone tried to shoot you and they aren't in fucking jail, Aspen," he growls.

"I told you, Dillon's working on it. I'm safe, Nash. Noah hired the best bodyguard in the state to help make sure I stay that way, and Brick and I are staying at his house until it's safe for me to go home. I'm not going to work or stepping a single toe outside."

"I don't like it."

"Yeah, well, neither do I. But having you roll into town to throw a fit isn't going to help anything. It's just going to stress me out even more. And I'm already stressed out, Nash. Noah is worse than you are," I complain.

My brother falls silent and then he curses. "Fine. I won't come. But I'm calling the sheriff."

"You're going to get yourself arrested."

"Good. He can put me in the cell with the motherfuckers who tried to shoot you."

I sigh, pinching the bridge of my nose. If Dillon doesn't catch them soon, I might get myself arrested just so I can get a little peace. Jail is probably way less stressful than Noah and Nash both trying to protect me.

By late afternoon, I'm bored out of my mind and ready to climb the walls. I call Jack instead and cajole him into sending supplies to me.

Noah said I couldn't go to work. But he never said work couldn't come to me. I need to bake. It soothes me.

I pop outside to let Giant know what's up. He sends one of his guys to the shop to help Jack load up what I need.

An hour later, someone knocks on the door.

I practically skip to the door.

"You said to expect a delivery," Giant says, his eyes wide. "This is an entire goddamn kitchen, Aspen."

"Oops?" I give him a cheeky grin, not the least bit sorry. Noah's kitchen is amazing, but it is not properly equipped for baking.

Giant grins back, shaking his head. "Where do you want all of this shit?"

"Kitchen, please." I start to slip under his arm to help him unload everything from the back of his employee's truck.

"Fuck, no," he says, stepping in front of me. "Back inside."

"Seriously?"

"Serious as a heart attack. Your man isn't banning my big ass from the arena because you broke the rules."

I scowl up at him. "You're way more fun when you're not in charge of me."

Amusement flashes in his eyes. "Mischief tells me the same thing," he says, referring to his wife, Bella. "But you'll thank me later."

I wrinkle my nose at him, making him laugh. But I give up on the idea of helping carry stuff in. Giant may be a madman more often than not, but he takes his job seriously. There's no way he's letting me step foot outside until Noah and Dillon give the all clear.

It takes him four trips to haul everything inside. He's wiping sweat by the time he finishes. "You really need all this shit?"

"Do you want fresh scones and cookies?"

"Uh, fuck yeah."

"Then yes, I need all this stuff."

He chuckles, holding his hands up. "I'm just going to take my big ass out of your kitchen and mind the business that earns me scones."

"Good choice."

He disappears down the hallway.

"Where are you going?" I call after him.

"Gotta piss!"

I shake my head, laughing. Giant doesn't ask for permission or forgiveness. He just does what he wants to do.

I start prowling through bags, pulling stuff out. Maybe Jack did send me a little bit too much stuff.

Footsteps sound behind me.

"Thanks for carrying everything in. I'll let you know when the scones are finished."

"Aspen."

I wheel around at the unfamiliar voice. My gaze lands on Troy, and my hands go lax. The container of blueberries plummets to the floor as shards of ice grow in my veins.

Chapter Twelve

Aspen

I stare at Troy, not breathing. He's here. Oh my God. He found me. He's going to kill me to keep me from identifying him.

I'll never see Noah again. I'll never get to hold the babies he's dying to have. Never own my own bakery. Never do any of the things I've put off, waiting until later. There won't *be* a later.

Tears well up from my soul, threatening to drown me in grief. But I don't have time to cry for all the things that could have--*should have*--been. If there's a chance of making it out of this. I have to find it.

For Noah.

For Nash.

For *me*.

My mind wheels and spins, trying to think my way out of this.

"I've already identified you," I say, voice shaking but firm. "The sheriff has photos of you and Silar fleeing the scene. Don't make it worse for yourself and throw away any hope of leniency."

"He found the camera?" Troy asks, his voice soft. Something almost like relief washes through his obsidian eyes. "That's good. I was worried he wouldn't."

I stare at him, uncertain.

He reads my confusion and smiles...attempts to smile. It's more of a grimace than anything. "You think I looked directly at that camera by accident?"

"Isn't that usually what happens?" I bite my lip as soon as the sarcastic response lands between us. Jeez. Why can't I ever just quit while I'm ahead?

Troy's lips curve into the semblance of a smile. "Point taken," he murmurs. "But I wanted to be caught."

"Why?" I demand, not sure I believe him. Not sure what to believe at this point. Why in the world would anyone want to get caught committing a felony?

"I wasn't supposed to be there in the first place." He lifts his hand, making me jump slightly. He notices but doesn't comment. He simply drops it back to his side. "Silar and I were friends a long time ago. We were not good kids. I got my shit together. He didn't. But before I got my shit together, I did some things I'm not proud of. Silar knows everything. He was there for all of it."

Where is Giant? Surely he's done peeing by now. I desperately want to look toward the hall to see if he's got a plan, but I don't. If Troy doesn't know he's here, I don't want to tip him off.

"So you felt like you owed it to him to break into the shop?" I ask, trying to keep him talking.

"Fuck no," he growls. "He came to me and said he needed help with something. I refused, but he threatened to release some very unfortunate photos." Troy sighs. "I agreed to go with him to get the goddamn photos back. I didn't know he had a gun until he tried to shoot you."

"So, what? You decided to look at the camera and hope you got caught to ease your conscience?" I ask. "You committed a felony, Troy."

"Believe me, I'm aware. But I didn't fucking sign up to shoot at anyone. If he's willing to kill you, what do you think he's willing to do to me?" he asks, one brow arched. "I'll take my chances with the law."

"Then why hide?"

"The photos," he mutters. "Silar wouldn't hand them over unless I skipped town with him. I think he knew I'd go straight to Dillon. I laid low with him until I got my hands on the photos, and then I bounced."

I eye him, not sure if I believe him or not. People do stupid things all the time, but this is an entirely new level of stupid. "What was in the photos?"

He presses his lips together, refusing to tell me...which is answer enough, I suppose. Whatever was in them is bad. Bad enough to make a felony like this seem like a viable alternative. I'm not sure I want to know the particulars. Men with money tend to think they can do whatever they want to whoever they want. It's disgusting.

Troy isn't a hero. He isn't a good guy, either. He's just one who hasn't learned yet that there is no atonement for some things. He's here because he thinks it balances the cosmic scale. It doesn't. Throwing himself at my mercy won't absolve him of whatever guilt he carries for what he did back then. It won't make him sleep better at night.

"If what you say is true, you need to tell the sheriff."

"I know." He blows out a breath. "I just wanted to talk to you first."

"You want me to plead your case."

He shrugs almost bashfully. He isn't bashful though. It's an act, one he's perfected in his life. If you're charming enough, people do what you want. Unfortunately for him, I'm not easily charmed.

"What was in the photos, Troy?"

"It doesn't matter. It was a long time ago."

"Will it matter to the girl in the photos?" I ask quietly.

He flinches, and I know I'm right. My stomach turns.

"Plead your own case," I say, disgusted. I'm not helping him. He doesn't deserve it.

"Aspen, please." He takes a step toward me.

"Take another fucking step and you're going to be eating through a straw, motherfucker," Giant growls, stepping into the kitchen from the hallway.

Troy wheels around to face him, shocked.

"Surprise, motherfucker." Giant grins at him, the gun in his hands steady. "Bet you didn't expect to see me, did you?"

Troy doesn't say anything. He just stares at him for a long moment. And then something in him...shifts. I'm not sure how else to describe it. It's eerie. One minute, he's just standing there, staring at Giant in silent resignation. The next, he blinks and spins toward me, his expression completely blank. He takes a step in my direction and then another, quickly closing the distance between us.

Giant doesn't hesitate. He fires.

I squeeze my eyes closed as Troy stumbles to a stop...and falls.

Chapter Thirteen

Noah

"Are you coming?" Colter asks, poking his head into my room through the passthrough door adjoining our rooms.

"What? Where?"

Colter's brows furrow as he steps fully into my room. "What the fuck is going on with you? You've been tense and distracted all day."

"I can't get ahold of Aspen." It's been hours since I last heard from her, and she's not the only one not answering. I've tried Cormac, Dillon, and Jack, too. No one is answering. No one has called me back yet, either.

The pit that opened in my stomach when I left this morning keeps yawning wider. Something is wrong. Aspen wouldn't ignore my calls given the situation. Neither would Cormac or Jack.

"Shit," Colter says, pulling his phone from his pocket. "I'll call Razor and see if he's heard anything." Razor Montgomery, his brother-in-law, runs in the same circles as Cormac and Dillon. And Razor's twin, Ryker, used to work for the CIA. If anyone can get me info, Razor can.

"Thanks," I mutter, pacing across the hotel room. There's not much room to accomplish it, but I need to move. I'm going stir crazy. Actually, I think I'm just losing it in general. Not knowing what's going on is stressing me the fuck out. Honestly, not being there right now is what's stressing me the fuck out.

Leaving her in the middle of this shit doesn't feel right. I should be with her right now, not seven hours away. Maybe this is why we never met when Nash and I played together. The universe or whatever knew she'd change my entire future. It knew as soon as I met her, my priorities would shift.

Hockey was my life once upon a time. Right now, it's the thing standing between me and the woman who makes me feel alive. I never thought I'd see the day I wanted something else more, but that day is here. It arrived the moment I met her, I think.

"Noah!" Colter shouts from his room. His tone sets my teeth on edge.

We meet at the door.

I know my intuition was right as soon as I see the look on his face. I grip the door handle, praying to God he doesn't tell me that she's hurt.

"He doesn't know exactly what happened," he says, "but Giant shot someone."

My knees threaten to buckle. "Tell me she's okay."

"As far as he knows," Colter says, clamping a hand on my shoulder. "She and Giant were at the Sheriff's Office for a few hours."

"Where the fuck are they now?" I growl.

"I don't know." He grimaces. "Razor was going to see what he could find out for you, but no one knows much right now."

"Jesus Christ." I drag my phone out of my pocket again, dialing Coach.

"What do you need, Diamante?"

"I need to go home," I growl. "There's an emergency." I quickly fill him in while Colter tosses my shit into my bag.

"Shit, yeah," Coach says. "Go. Do you need a lift to the airport?"

"I'll catch an Uber."

"Keep us posted."

I disconnect and grab my bag from Colter, slinging it over my shoulder.

"I'll call you as soon as Razor calls me," he tells me. "I'll also ask Reid to check with Wren too, see if she's heard anything." Reid's wife is a lawyer. Her brother is a judge in Silver Spoon Falls. If anyone can get me information on the shooting, she can. "Go get your girl."

I duck out of the room, jogging toward the elevator.

"Where the fuck are you going?" Atlas asks, poking his head out of Devlin's room.

"Home."

"What the fuck?" Atlas steps out into the hallway behind me. "Why?"

I don't bother answering as I round the corner. Colter will fill him in. I take the stairs instead of waiting for the elevator. I'm too goddamn jittery to stand there patiently, cooling my heels while the elevator takes its sweet time getting to me.

Five minutes later, I'm pacing the lobby, waiting for my Uber when the doors slide open.

My gaze skims over the curvy woman hurrying into the hotel, already dismissing her as I glance back down at my phone. And then I jerk my head up, doing a double take. She looks just like...

"Aspen?"

I've officially lost it. I'm seeing shit that isn't possible. She's in Silver Spoon Falls, not Oklahoma City. Yet she's standing in the hotel lobby. What the fuck?

"Hey, Superstar," she says, smirking at me. "Did you miss me?"

I drop my bag, crossing to her in three steps.

She squeals as I lift her off her feet into my arms, crashing my mouth down on hers. Her arms twine around my neck, a soft laugh burbling from her lips.

"How are you here right now?" I ask, not entirely convinced that I'm not just imagining the whole thing. She's in my arms and she feels real, but I was in hell not even thirty seconds ago. Forgive me for doubting heaven just appeared before me.

"Did you know Giant's best friend owns a jet?" She looks at me with wide eyes. "You guys should really look into borrowing it to fly instead of using the bus. It's way faster."

"You borrowed a private jet to fly here?"

"No. Giant borrowed it to get me here." She touches my cheek, smiling. "He's outside, getting my bags."

"Giant's here?"

She nods. "Dillon thought it would be best if we left town."

"He shot someone."

Her eyes widen. "You know?"

"I've been going out of my fucking mind," I growl, scooping my bag from the floor without putting her down. I carry her toward the elevator, not giving a shit who sees us. "What the hell happened?"

"It's a long story."

"I've got time," I say, stabbing the button for the elevator.

Naturally, the doors immediately slide open.

Aspen makes a face at me.

I ignore it and stab the button for the fourth floor before backing her up against the wall. "Talk, Dimples."

"I wanted to bake so I convinced Jack to send me supplies. I guess Troy was watching the shop because he showed up in the kitchen while Giant was going pee. He tried to convince me to plead his case for him because he claims that Silar was blackmailing him and that's the only reason he was there. But when I found out why Silar was blackmailing him, I refused. He didn't like that much. I guess he decided to gamble with his life?" She shrugs before rambling on. "I'm not sure what he was thinking, honestly. But he started rushing toward me, so Giant shot him."

"He's dead?"

"He probably wishes he were," she mutters darkly. "I told Dillon everything. But he'll survive the gunshot wound. Giant shot him in the shoulder."

"I suddenly have a pressing need to get arrested."

She groans, dropping her head against my shoulder. "Nash said the same thing."

"You talked to Nash?"

"After you left this morning," she whispers.

"Hold that thought," I mutter when the elevator shudders to a stop on the fourth floor. The doors slide open.

Of course it slides open to half my teammates standing on the opposite side. They take one look at the way I'm holding her, and the catcalls commence.

"Stow it!" Colter barks, meeting my gaze as Aspen tries to squirm out of my arms. "You good, Noah?"

"Perfect," I growl, trying to keep Aspen still before my dick gets any harder.

Colter jerks his head in a nod, relief in his gaze. "We're taking the stairs, people."

"We're on the fourth floor," Atlas complains.

"Then your big ass better get to walking."

Atlas flips him off, earning laughs from the rest of the team as I carry Aspen out of the elevator. They all head toward the stairs. Colter hangs back for a minute.

"Glad to see you're okay," he murmurs to Aspen.

"Thanks," she whispers.

"I'm bunking with Atlas tonight." He meets my gaze.

"Thanks, brother."

He gives me a chin lift and then heads toward the elevators.

"What was that about?"

"Adjoining rooms."

A blush creeps up Aspen's cheeks. "Oh," she whispers.

I chuckle, carrying her down the hall toward my room. We don't speak again until we're over the threshold. I drop my bag and then deposit her on the bed, crawling over her. "I've been losing my mind worrying about you."

"I'm sorry." She reaches out, placing her palm against my cheek in apology. "I didn't want to tell you any of this over the phone because I knew you would worry. I figured if I waited until I got here, you'd worry less." She grimaces. "I didn't count on someone else telling you before the plane landed."

"I only found out ten minutes before you got here. I was on my way to the airport."

"You were flying home? Noah, you have a game."

I reach over my head, pulling my shirt off. "I realized something."

"What?"

"I want a future with you more than I want hockey."

"You don't have to choose between us," she says. "I'd never ask you to do that."

"I can spend the rest of my life with the woman I can't live without, or I can spend half of it on the road without her. I've had enough of the latter and not nearly enough of the former." I brush my lips against hers. "I'm not asking permission, baby. I'm telling you that this is how it's going to be. When my contract expires, I'm done."

"When does your contract expire?"

"At the end of the year."

"I just talked Nash into not giving up hockey, now you want to give it up," she frets.

"I'm not Nash, Dimples. I'm not sacrificing anything. I'm just beginning to realize that my heart isn't in the game anymore. That's the worst kind of player to have on a team. My spot should go to someone willing to eat, sleep, and breathe hockey. That's not me anymore." I press my lips to her furrowed brows. "I'm filling a slot that some other motherfucker dreams of holding. It should go to him."

"I don't like it."

"You don't have to like it." I grin at her. "You aren't the boss of me."

She growls and pushes against my chest, forcing me onto my back. "We'll see about that, Noah Diamante." She clambers over me, straddling my hips. "I bet I can make you do whatever I want."

She's not wrong about that. Especially if she keeps straddling me like she is.

"You better finish telling me what happened today, Dimples. In about five minutes, you won't be able to say anything but my name."

"Troy told Dillon where to find Silar, so he's in jail, too."

"Getting arrested is looking better and better."

"You can't get arrested. I promised Nash that you were going to look out for me. You can't do that from jail, Noah."

"You really talked to him?" I ask, more surprised by that than anything.

"I did," she whispers. "He knows everything now."

"Everything?"

"I mean, I left out the part about your tattoo, but I can call him back if you want..." she says, shifting as if she's going to reach into her pocket for her phone.

I grab her, flipping her onto her back beneath me.

She laughs out loud, her eyes shining with happiness as she stares up at me. "He knows everything, Noah." Her expression softens. "I think we're both going to be okay now."

"Yeah?"

She nods.

"Yeah, you are," I agree, leaning down to capture her lips with mine. I kiss her long and deep, sealing my vow. She will be okay now. My new goal in life is making sure she's more than okay every day. I made her brother a promise, after all.

I fully intend to keep it.

"I love you," she whispers as we strip each other bare.

"Not nearly as much as I love you."

"Lies," she moans as I lift her legs over my shoulders, skimming my lips up the inside of her thigh. "All lies."

"I bet I can convince you otherwise, Dimples."

"Do it."

I bury my face in her center, taking us both to heaven all over again.

Epilogue

Aspen

Three Years Later

"Mommy!" Owen squeals my name, scurrying across the shop as fast as his little legs will carry him. "Mommy!"

I step out from behind the counter, scooping him up into my arms. "Hi, baby boy," I croon, pressing kisses to his adorable little face. "I missed you today."

He laughs, placing his palms against my cheeks. His green eyes shine with happiness. "Misseded you." He squirms for me to put him down.

I give him another kiss and then set him back on his feet. He immediately takes off toward the play area we set up on the far side of the shop to keep kids occupied while their parents enjoy a peaceful coffee.

At two, he's always on the move. He's been the same way since he was born. He's just like Noah in that way. My husband spent his life on the ice, exhausting himself every day. Now that he's retired from the AHL, he has an unlimited supply of energy and far too much time on his hands. He teaches a little league team here in town. He also opened a gym last year. He spends a lot of his time torturing other people with physical activity.

It works well for me because it means he's not torturing me with physical activity. I prefer to keep mine limited to the bedroom. And the occasional treadmill. He wants to traverse mountains and run. That does not sound like a good time to me.

"Damn, Dimples," he says, stalking across the shop toward me with a smirk on his face. "You look good enough to eat."

"Noah," I chastise, swatting his hands as he reaches for me. "We agreed you weren't going to make inappropriate comments in public anymore."

"This isn't public, Aspen. It's your shop."

"And it's full of people," I point out.

He glances around like he's just noticing them for the first time. He probably is. When I'm around, his eyes are always on me. He's pretty oblivious to everyone else...right up until he thinks they're trying to flirt with me anyway.

And then he sees them all too well. He's kicked more men out of here than I can count.

They're used to it by now. Honestly, I think they have a pool going to see who he kicks out the most. I have no idea who is winning at this point. It's hard to keep up when he kicks someone out at least once a day.

"They can leave if they don't like it," he says with a shrug, dragging me into his arms.

I laugh quietly, resting my head against his chest. "You can't kick out the entire shop, Noah."

"Don't tempt me. You look beautiful today." He rubs my belly. "How's my baby doing?"

"He's good."

"She."

"No."

"You can't just say no, Aspen. We're having a girl."

"I refuse to accept this." Honestly, I've resigned myself to the fact that we're having a little girl. I'm excited to meet her in a few months. But I do not envy the next fifty years of her life. She's going to need a spine of steel to deal with her daddy, her uncle, and her big brother. They'll have her wrapped in bubble wrap and surrounded by an army.

"Accept it." He drops a kiss on my lips. "You're carrying my baby girl."

I shake my head, smiling. He's as ridiculous as ever. And I love him more than ever for it. The last three years have been the best three years of my life. I never imagined happiness like this existed for me. But every day is brighter than the last with him.

My heart is full, and it grows fuller every year.

"Your brother will be here soon," he reminds me. "Are you ready?"

"For hockey?" I eye him sideways. "I'm always ready for hockey, Noah."

He grins at me, his eyes alight with humor. "Are you ready to have your brother in the same state as you again, smartass."

Nash was traded to the Dallas Stars at the start of the season. I know he did it to be closer to me, but this time...I don't mind because he isn't coming alone. He's bringing his wife and baby with him. I'm not the only one who has healed and changed. He has too. In so many ways.

He's still an overprotective bully. But he's an amazing father and he idolizes his wife. He's happy. Happier than he's ever been. And he isn't giving up hockey to move here. He wants his son to grow up close to mine. He wants his wife to have family close when he's away. I don't blame him for that.

"I'm ready," I say, meaning it with all my heart. For the first time in a long time...I'm ready. We're ready. It's a big step forward.

Noah smiles at me, pulling me into a hug. "I'm proud of you, Dimples," he whispers in my ear. "You're going to love having him here again."

"I am," I whisper, meaning that, too.

"Then move your ass, baby," he says, nipping my throat. "We've got to hit the road if we're going to make it to Dallas for the game."

"It's nine in the morning, Noah."

"Mmhmm. And between you and Owen, we're going to have to stop nine thousand times to pee. So if we don't leave now, we aren't going to make it in time for the game."

He has a point. I do have to pee a lot.

"Let me get my stuff and let Emilia know we're leaving."

"I'll round up the boy." He drops a kiss on my lips and then starts to pull away.

"Hey, Noah?" I place my hand on his arm, halting him.

"Yeah?"

"Thank you," I whisper.

He cocks his head to the side. "For what?"

"For everything."

His expression softens as he pulls me back into his arms. "Thank you for everything too," he murmurs against my lips. "I love you, Dimples."

"I love you too."

AUTHOR'S NOTE

Thank you so much for reading Aspen and Noah's story! If you enjoyed it, please leave a review!

Gabbi's Goalie, Atlas's story, releases in November. You can pre-order it here

SILVER SPOON FALCONS

What we wanted: professional athletes. What we got: stick-wielding madmen who look good in blue, play hard, and love harder. It's a good thing this is Silver Spoon Falls because these hunky hockey players fit right in.

Welcome the Falcons to the roster! These over-the-top athletes are about to play the most important game of all: the game of love. And the sassy, curvy women of Silver Spoon Falls have no intention of going down without a fight.

Let the games begin!

Check out the series: https://www.amazon.com/dp/B0C6KGFG8H

- Allie's Enforcer by Loni Ree (June) - https://www.amazon.com/gp/product/B0B9HY6GJJ

- Leia's Playmaker by Nichole Rose (July) - https://mybook.to/LeiaFalcons

- Carlie's Coach by Loni Ree (August) - https://www.amazon.com/gp/product/B0BRYMJGRL

- Aspen's Defense by Nichole Rose (September) - https://mybook.to/AspensDefense

- Lana's Winger by Lonie Ree (October) - https://www.amazon.com/gp/product/B0BRYM4YFZ

- Gabbi's Goalie by Nichole Rose (November) - https://mybook.to/GabbisGoalie

RUINED: THE COMPLETE SERIES

Redemption never hurt so good.

The Valentino brothers rule the city of Chicago with closed fists and iron wills. But even kings fall. And the curvy women meant for them are about to drop these crime bosses to their knees. The story doesn't start with them, though. It starts with Nico, the brother who escaped a life chained to the mafia.

For the first time ever, get all four books in the series in one giant bundle with a brand-new bonus scene.

Physical Science – One twin wants to kill her. The other wants to worship her. When the dust settles, will love prove triumphant for the curvy young student caught between the professor of her dreams and the dangerous mob boss who haunts her nightmares?

Wrecked – In a city where crime doesn't sleep, Rafe Valentino is a waking nightmare. But even kings fall. And this king promises to leave behind a crater when he falls for the curvy sister of his enemy. But she's keeping secrets that just might burn his empire to the ground with him. Will the powerful connection between them survive the truth, or will his enemies use it to destroy them both?

Wanton – A life in hell was the sacrifice Luca Valentino made to keep his brothers alive. And there's nothing he won't do to see the job through...even if it means seducing the enemy. But he never intended to fall for her. Now, the woman who holds the key to his future is in chains in his bedroom, and their families are on the brink of war. Can he win her heart and her trust in time to save them both?

Wicked – They say those with the power make the

rules...but when Gabriel Valentino meets Genesis Burbank, the rules go out the window. The curvy bombshell refuses to bend to his will, and he isn't used to losing. Especially when it matters. He'll do whatever it takes to possess her. Even if he has to break her to claim her.

If you enjoy morally gray heroes, dark romance, and fiery heroines, you'll love the Valentino brothers and their curvy women!

RUINED: THE COMPLETE SERIES releases on all retailers on September 26th! Pre-order here.

FOLLOW NICHOLE

Like free books? Me too! Sign-up for my mailing list at http://authornicholerose.com/newsletter to stay up-to-date on all new releases and for exclusive giveaways and freebies!

Want to connect with me and other readers? Join Nichole Rose's Book Beauties on Facebook!

facebook.com/AuthorNicholeRose/

instagram.com/AuthorNicholeRose

twitter.com/AuthNicholeRose

bookbub.com/authors/nichole-rose

tiktok.com/@authornicholerose

INSTALOVE BOOK CLUB

The Instalove Book Club is now in session!

Get the inside scoop from your favorite instalove authors, meet new authors to love, and snag a free book and bonus content from featured authors every month. The Instalove Book Club newsletter goes out once per week!

Join the Club: http://instalovebookclub.com

NICHOLE'S BOOK BEAUTIES

Want to connect with Nichole and other readers? We're building a girl gang! Join Nichole Rose's Book Beauties on Facebook for fun, games, and behind-the-scenes exclusives!

ALSO BY NICHOLE ROSE

Her Alpha Series

Her Alpha Daddy Next Door

Her Alpha Boss Undercover

Her Alpha's Secret Baby

Her Alpha Protector

Her Date with an Alpha

Her Alpha: The Complete Series

Her Bride Series

His Future Bride

His Stolen Bride

His Secret Bride

His Curvy Bride

His Captive Bride

His Blushing Bride

His Bride: The Complete Series

Claimed Series

Possessing Liberty

Teaching Rowan

Claiming Caroline

Kissing Kennedy

Claimed: The Complete Series

Love on the Clock Series

Adore You

Hold You

Keep You

Protect You

Love on the Clock: The Complete Series

The Billionaires' Club

The Billionaire's Big Bold Weakness

The Billionaire's Big Bold Wish

The Billionaire's Big Bold Woman

The Billionaire's Big Bold Wonder

The Billionaires' Club: The Complete Series

Playing for Keeps

Cutie Pie

Ice Breaker
Ice Prince
Ice Giant
Cold as Ice
Ice Storm

Full-Length Titles

Crash into You
Fight for You (coming soon)
Kill for You (coming soon)

The Second Generation

A Blushing Bride for Christmas

Love Bites

Come Undone
Dripping Pearls

Echoes of Forever

His Christmas Miracle
Taken by the Hitman
Wicked Saint

<u>The Ruined Trilogy</u>

Physical Science

Wrecked

Wanton

Wicked

Ruined: The Complete Series

<u>Illicit Love Series</u>

Irresistible

Irrevocable

Irreplaceable

Irredeemable

<u>Destination Romance</u>

Romancing the Cowboy

Beach House Beauty

<u>Standalone Titles</u>

A Touch of Summer

Black Velvet

His Secret Obsession

Dirty Boy

Naughty Little Elf

Tempted by December

Devil's Deceit
A Bride for the Beast (writing with Fern Fraser)
A Hero for Her
Pretty Little Mess
Dear Mr. Dad Bod

<u>Easy on Me</u>
Easy Ride
Easy Surrender

<u>One Night with You</u>
Falling Hard
Model Behavior
Learning Curve
Angel Kisses

<u>Silver Spoon MC</u>
The Surgeon
The Heir
The Lawyer
The Prodigy
The Bodyguard
Silver Spoon MC Collection: Nichole's Crew

Silver Spoon Falls

Xavier's Kitten

Callum's Hope

Snow's Prince

Aurora's Knight

Silver Spoon Falcons

Leia's Playmaker

Aspen's Defense (coming soon)

Gabbi's Goalie (coming soon)

writing with Loni Ree as Loni Nichole

Dillon's Heart

Razor's Flame

Ryker's Reward

Zane's Rebel

Oral Arguments

Grizz's Passion

Garrett's Obsession

ABOUT NICHOLE ROSE

Nichole Rose writes filthy romance for curvy readers. Her books feature headstrong, sassy women and the alpha males who consume them. From grumpy detectives to country boys with attitude to instalove and over-the-top declarations, nothing is off-limits.

Nichole is sure to have a steamy, sweet story just right for everyone. She fully believes the world is ugly enough without trying to fit falling in love into a one-size-fits-all box.

When not writing, Nichole enjoys fine wine, cute shoes, and everything supernatural. She is happily married to the love of her life and is a proud mama to the world's most ridiculous fur-babies. She and her husband live in Arkansas.

You can learn more about Nichole and her books at authornicholerose.com.

facebook.com/AuthorNicholeRose/

instagram.com/AuthorNicholeRose

twitter.com/AuthNicholeRose

bookbub.com/authors/nichole-rose

tiktok.com/@authornicholerose

9 798223 846550